'I still say it would be easier with a fishing rod,' said Callum.

Gran gave him a look. 'He is a polar bear. He doesn't fish with a rod. He uses his paws.'

'I don't think polar bears normally fish with snorkels and masks either,' said Lucy.

Gran frowned. 'It's different in the Arctic,' she said.

'And why use the boat?' Lucy continued. 'Wouldn't it be easier to fish off the rocks?'

Gran sighed a loud sigh. 'Do you want to help on this mission or not? And you should know never to fish off those rocks because there is always a danger of being cut off by the tide.'

Maya saw Lucy and Callum glance at each other. She felt bad. It was obvious that neither of them were enjoying this and nor was Mister P. But when Gran put her mind to something, nothing could stop her.

On Gran's instructions, Mister P leant over the side of the boat and put his face in the water.

For Granny Hazel, with love—MF
For my Mum and Dad—DR

OXFORD
UNIVERSITY PRESS

Great Clarendon Street, Oxford OX2 6DP

Oxford University Press is a department of the University of Oxford.
It furthers the University's objective of excellence in research, scholarship,
and education by publishing worldwide. Oxford is a registered trade mark of
Oxford University Press in the UK and in certain other countries

First published 2019

British Library Cataloguing in Publication Data
Data available

ISBN: 978-0-19-276655-7

1 3 5 7 9 10 8 6 4 2

Printed in Great Britain

Paper used in the production of this book is a natural,
recyclable product made from wood grown in sustainable forests.
The manufacturing process conforms to the environmental
regulations of the country of origin.

ME AND MISTER P

MAYA'S STORM

WRITTEN BY
MARIA FARRER

ILLUSTRATED BY
DANIEL RIELEY

OXFORD
UNIVERSITY PRESS

CHAPTER 1
LOSING YOUR MARBLES

From her bed in Lighthouse Cottage, Maya could hear the sea. Sometimes massive waves rolled in, booming and crashing against the rocks. Other times gentle ripples whispered along the shoreline.

The storms still scared Maya, but not as much as they used to. These days she mostly felt safe and secure in her seaside home; safe with her Mum and Dad, safe with her big brother Max and her sister, Iris, and safe with Granny Anne who lived in an old cottage at the edge of the village. This was Maya's new family.

Maya once had another family in a country
far away across the sea. When she tried to
remember them she felt an emptiness in her
tummy, like a hole, and it made her sad and
scared. Granny Anne had taken her to the beach
and found a pebble with a hole right the way
through the centre. 'Losing something special
sometimes feels like a hole,' she said. She held up
the pebble so Maya could see the light shining
through the hole. 'But if you keep looking
forward, you will always find light at the end
of the tunnel.' Gran had wrapped the pebble
in a square of blue velvet and put it in Maya's
box of memories. Now,
whenever Maya felt sad,
she unwrapped the pebble
and held it up to the light
until she felt better.

Maya's box of
memories was made of
wood and had a sliding lid

with a seagull carved on the top. It was Maya's
first ever present from Gran and she loved
to close her eyes and run her fingers over the
ridges of wood to feel the wings and head and
beak of the bird. Maya had come to Lighthouse
Cottage with nothing, and her box of memories
had become her treasure chest. Over the years,
she and Gran had filled it with memories of
every part of her life since she'd arrived: shells,
fossils and feathers, birthday cards, pencils and
badges, and stacks of little memory notes, each
one carefully illustrated with a picture. This was
Maya's new life, it was her very own, and no one
could take it away from her.

'You must learn to treasure
your memories,' said Gran,
'because when you get to my
age they start to disappear.
Soon you'll have to look after
my memories as well as your
own.'

'Where do they disappear to?' asked Maya.

Gran clicked her fingers. 'Into thin air!'

'Why?' asked Maya.

'I don't know. Maybe the brain gets tired and forgets to hold onto them.'

Maya laughed and so did Gran.

Mum and Dad didn't laugh. They didn't like it when Gran's brain got tired. It made them stressed and worried. Dad said Gran was losing her marbles. Maya wondered what that had to do with anything.

'She's getting old,' said Mum. 'We have to accept that things are going to change.'

Maya refused to listen. She wasn't ready for change. She'd had quite enough change in her life already.

CHAPTER 2
THE CALM
BEFORE THE STORM

It was late and everyone else in the family had gone to bed. Maya knew she should be asleep, but the wind was blowing and making her restless. She sat at the table in her bedroom and hoped Mum and Dad wouldn't notice the light under her door. She put the finishing touches to Gran's party invitation. Gran would be seventy-five in August and Maya had decided she was going to do something special for Gran as a way of saying thank you for all the special things that Gran had done for her. They'd been discussing plans for ages. Tomorrow she would take the finished invitation to Gran for a quick check to make sure she hadn't forgotten anything. It was going to be brilliant and she couldn't wait.

She jotted a quick memory note for her box.

Getting ready for the best
summer holiday EVER

She added some pictures of sea, sun, and sand.

Maya loved pictures and all her memory notes were decorated with drawings to help bring them to life. It was hard to believe now, but when she'd first arrived she could hardly speak or understand a single word people were saying. For a long time she'd been afraid even to open her mouth. It was Gran who had helped her learn, first with pictures and then with speaking and writing. Mum, Dad, Max, and Iris had helped too, but they didn't have quite so much time or patience—and they weren't as good at drawing.

She flopped backwards onto her bed and stared up at the ceiling. *Summer*, she thought. *Gran and me, the beach and the sea.* It wasn't that she didn't enjoy school, it's just that she enjoyed the holidays more. She wished Mum and Dad could have a holiday too, but they were always hard at work.

Dad was a Coastguard and his job was to rescue anyone in danger along the cliffs and seashore. He worked shifts and when he wasn't working or sleeping, he was helping Mum with running the Lighthouse Holiday Cottages. The summer was the busiest time for both of them. 'Full of tourists who don't know what they are doing,' Dad always said.

The lighthouse was close to the cottages and Maya could see it now—its beam of light pulsing out across the sea—two flashes every three seconds. Her window rattled and the curtain billowed in the breeze. She got up to close it and rested her forehead against the

windowpane, watching the waves rise and fall
as the light swept over the water.

It was a clear evening, but Dad said the weather
was changing—and Dad was always right about
the weather. As she pulled the curtain closed
she stopped. She squinted into the distance. She
thought she'd seen something—a dark shape—
way, way out. She blinked and scanned the
horizon carefully

    . . . nothing

        . . . she must have been mistaken.

Maya clambered into bed and tried to go to
sleep, but now she was even more restless than
before. She was sure she'd seen something.
She threw back the covers and returned to the
window, pressing her nose against the glass. It was
darker now—harder to see. Then her heart gave
a jolt. There it was again. Closer. It looked like a
small boat. Maya waited for the next pulse of light
to illuminate the sea. The waves rose and fell.
It was hard to be certain.

Then it came into view again. A small boat with someone **very large** in it! Someone wearing a heavy white coat! The boat rose on the crest of a wave and then disappeared into the shadows.

Maya ran to wake Mum and Dad. The lighthouse wasn't here for nothing—it was here as a warning to boats and ships about the rocky headland. There shouldn't be anyone that close. It wasn't just the rocks you *could* see, but the ones like sharks' teeth *beneath* the water that were dangerous.

'Mum, Dad, QUICK! I think there's someone in trouble.'

Maya shook Dad to make sure he was properly awake.

'What? Where?' Dad sat up and grabbed his binoculars. He and Mum hurried to the window. But, as the three of them searched the water, there was nothing to be seen except the inky black waves.

'I promise I saw something,' said Maya. 'It was a small boat and it had someone in it— someone big.'

Dad smiled and shook his head. 'Water can play tricks on us at night,' he said, giving her a hug. 'There's many a time I've thought I've seen boats or dolphins and it's just been the dark of the water and the white tops of waves breaking out at sea. Or maybe it was just a dream.'

Maya shook her head. She knew she'd been wide awake, but now she felt foolish.

Dad scanned the sea again. 'You were right to

wake us. It's always better to be safe than sorry. Now let's get you back to bed.'

'But I can't sleep,' said Maya.

Mum and Dad took Maya back to her room and tucked her into bed. Dad picked up Maya's invitation for Gran's party.

'This is a lovely idea of yours, Maya,' said Dad. 'I do hope Gran will be up to it. She's not been quite herself recently.'

'Of course she'll be up to it. She's looking forward to it.'

Mum perched on the edge of the bed and took Maya's hand. 'I know all this business with

Granny Anne is a bit unsettling,' said Mum, 'but you mustn't worry about it too much.'

'I'm not,' said Maya.

'I've reminded Gran—twice—that you're going round there tomorrow, so she should remember.'

'Mum,' said Maya. 'STOP FUSSING.' Maya turned over to face the wall. Sometimes Mum went way over the top with her worrying.

Dad bent to give Maya a kiss. 'No more mystery boat sightings, please.'

Maya pretended to be asleep and waited until Mum and Dad had gone before creeping to the window one last time. Tomorrow, she decided, she'd go down to the beach with Gran and see if there was any sign of anything being washed up on the shore.

CHAPTER 3
FACING YOUR FEARS

Typical! Why did it always decide to rain as soon as the holidays started? Big, fat raindrops splatted against the window and it was hard to see where the clouds stopped and the sea began. She could hear the waves crashing on the rocks below and Mum and Dad thumping about downstairs, getting all the sheets and towels ready to do the changeover from one lot of guests to the next at the holiday cottages.

Maya pulled on her clothes, ran downstairs, and grabbed a glass of milk and an apple. Gran always had a proper breakfast waiting so there was no point in filling herself up before she left. She put on her waterproofs and headed towards Gran's house, the invitation in her pocket. When she arrived the door of Home Cottage stood wide open and rainwater was pooling on the floor.

'Gran? Gran!' Maya called.

She did a quick search of the garden and then went into the house. Maya loved Gran's house. Old fishing nets and anchors hung on the wall, cabinets stood tall, filled with shells and driftwood Gran had collected from nearby beaches, and every surface was covered in photos and paintings of Gran's life from childhood to now. Gran had been brought up in this house and had never moved, even when she married Grandpa Ted.

'Granny Anne,' Maya called again, louder this time.

There was no sign of Gran and no sign of breakfast either.

Mrs Ross came round from next door. 'If you're looking for your granny, she went out about an hour ago. Said she was off to the beach—though what she thinks she's doing going to the beach in this weather I have no idea.'

'Why didn't she wait for me?' said Maya. 'She knew I was coming.'

'Time and tide wait for no man,' said Mrs Ross. 'And you know your grandmother.'

It didn't surprise Maya that Gran had gone out in the rain. What did surprise her was that Gran would NEVER go out when Maya was coming over, especially if it was breakfast time. Maya took the invitation out of her pocket and left it on the table. It would be safer here at the cottage. She closed the front door, zipped up her waterproof, and jogged towards the rocky path that led down to the beach. As she reached the top, she saw an unmistakable figure hurrying towards her wearing old baggy shorts and an oilskin coat.

Granny Anne was small and wiry, with long grey wispy hair and a face that reminded Maya of a walnut. Gran often said that every wrinkle was the sign of an adventure. Maya decided Gran must have had plenty of adventures. As soon as she saw Maya, she stopped. She was puffing from her walk up the steep slope, and was hopping from foot to foot, the way she always did when she was worried or excited.

'Hello Maya. Oh goodness me. I'm so pleased you're here. I need your help.'

'My help?' Maya's heart beat a little faster. 'Why? What's up?'

'I've found something down on the beach. A boat!'

Maya's mind raced back to last night and what she'd seen—or thought she'd seen—from the window of her bedroom. 'Have you spoken to Mum or Dad this morning?' Maya asked.

Gran stopped and looked a little confused. 'Have I? No, I don't think so. Why?'

'Nothing,' said Maya. 'I just thought they might have mentioned . . .'

But Granny Anne had turned and was already half walking, half trotting back down the path. 'Come on, come on,' she said. 'We need to get back before anyone else gets to the beach. We need to *investigate*.' Gran managed to make the word *investigate* sound mysterious and exciting. Maya grinned. This is what the summer was about.

As soon as they reached the beach, Maya shrugged off her coat, flipped off her canvas shoes, and hurried along the wet sand. Lumpy seaweed, washed up by the storm, squelched between her toes.

'There! Look!' said Gran.

Ahead, Maya could see an old wooden boat lying on its side on the sand. It looked like the boat she'd seen last night—it must be. Where else would it have appeared from? She swallowed and hurried on after Gran.

'And look at this,' Gran continued, crouching down and pointing to the most enormous footprint beside the boat.

Maya examined the print closely. There wasn't just one, there were loads and they didn't look like any footprint Maya had ever seen before. They were bigger than a dinner plate and had five sharp claw marks across the top.

'Have *you* made these, Gran?' said Maya, suddenly suspicious that this might be one of Gran's elaborate jokes. Gran could make up the most incredible stories.

Gran looked cross. 'I most certainly have NOT.'

'Hmmm.' Maya inspected them again. 'So what do you think they could be?'

'Well I'm no expert, but if you want me to take a guess, I'd say these are the footprints of a very large animal.'

This *must* be a joke. Gran *must* have spoken to Mum and Dad, Maya felt sure of it. But as her eyes followed the line of paw prints up the beach toward the cave, she started to feel slightly uneasy. She tried to picture more clearly what she'd seen in the boat last night. It had looked very large . . . and furry. She had thought it was a *person* wearing some kind of warm coat, but could it have been an animal? An animal with exceptionally large paws? A shiver went down her spine.

'I think we should go and take a look,' said Gran.

Maya wasn't so enthusiastic. 'Perhaps we should call someone—like someone who knows about these things?'

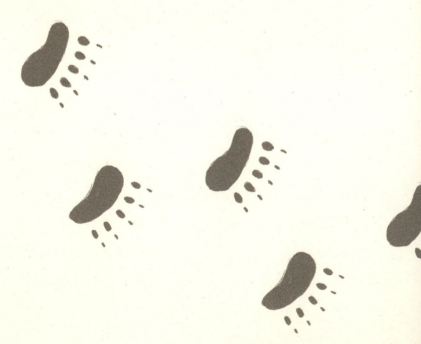

'Don't be such a spoilsport,' said Gran. 'We don't anyone stealing our discovery. And who would we call?' Gran took Maya's hand, and held it tightly as they tracked the prints up the soft sand to the mouth of the cave. Maya looked over her shoulder and couldn't help noticing how tiny her own footprints seemed in comparison. She scanned the sand for any sign of paw prints walking back OUT of the cave. There were none. So if, IF something had gone into the cave, it must still be in there. Maya hesitated—she wasn't at all sure she wanted to go any further.

'We're not stopping now,' said Gran. 'We must be bold and brave. If there is something to be found, we must find it.'

'Must we?' said Maya, still holding back.

'Always face your fears,' said Gran and took a deep breath. 'Are you ready? On the count of three . . .

ONE . . .

TWO . . .

TWO AND A HALF . . .

TWO AND THREE QUARTERS . . .

THREE!'

They looked at each other then stepped
into the blackness of the cave.

CHAPTER 4
SHEDDING LIGHT ON THE SITUATION

The cave was deep and dark and smelt of fish and sea.

'Hello?' said Gran in a quiet, sing-song voice. The sound echoed round the silence of the cave. 'Is there anybody there?'

They waited. There was no answer.

Maya hung back just behind Gran. Caves scared her. She didn't like darkness.

Gran felt around and pulled a small torch from her pocket. 'Let's shed some light on this situation,' she said. She moved the light slowly around the cave. Maya gasped and pulled at

Gran's sleeve. Right at the back, in the darkest corner, was something large and lumpy and pale.

'What is it?' whispered Maya.

They tiptoed towards it. Close up, the lumpiness looked more like a shaggy, dirty, sea-weedy heap of fur. Maya wondered if it was the coat she had seen in the boat.

Gran put a finger to her lips and leant forward. A soft, regular rumbling sound was coming from the heap. She and Gran looked at each other.

'Sounds like snoring,' said Granny Anne. 'It must be alive!'

HARR-UMPH

The creature moved. Maya leapt out of her skin and tried to run, but Gran held on to her. Two bright eyes sprang open and stared straight at them.

'There's no need to be scared,' said Gran, her voice soft and gentle.

Maya wasn't sure if Gran was talking to her

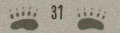

or the animal. The words echoed in Maya's head. *There's no need to be scared. There's no need to be scared.* Granny Anne had said that to Maya so many times; when Maya had first arrived, when she'd refused to leave the safety of her bedroom, when she hadn't wanted to go to school. But this was different. This was a huge animal in the back of a dark cave. Maybe it *was* scared.

The eyes stared up at Maya and she took a step forward and crouched down. She reached out and let her fingers touch the damp fur.

'Hello,' she said. 'What are you doing here?'

The animal lifted its head.

'I think it's a polar bear,' said Maya. 'A real live polar bear. In our cave!'

Gran had shifted the beam of the torch so it was shining on an old, brown, rather soggy-looking suitcase just close to the bear's front paw. Tied around the handle was a label, but the writing was so smudged that it was hard to read. It looked like a name, all dripping and inky.

'Mister P?' breathed Maya. She turned the label over. On the other side . . . Gran shone the beam of the torch at the smudged writing . . . Maya's hand flew to her mouth.

It was Maya's very own address. She slipped the label off the suitcase and put it in her pocket. She wanted to examine it more closely in the daylight.

Gran sat down on a large rock and rubbed her eyes as if the vision of the polar bear with a suitcase might go away. 'Tell me I'm not imagining this,' she said to Maya. 'Tell me I'm not going completely mad.'

'You're not imagining it. I can see the bear as clearly as you can.'

'A polar bear with a suitcase,' said Gran as if trying to convince herself. Then she laughed. 'Now this is beginning to feel like a proper adventure. Why don't you open the case and see what's inside? After all, your address is on it.'

Maya wasn't sure. 'It's a bit rude opening someone's private property, isn't it? Do you think he'll mind?'

'We'll soon find out,' said Gran.

I'll soon find out more like, thought Maya, as she bent down and went to unclip the two catches.

The bear watched closely as Maya lifted the lid. Gran held the torch for Maya to see. Maya examined the strange selection of objects. It wasn't at all what she'd expected: a football, some headphones, a mouth organ, and other unusual polar bear bits and pieces. It looked like his own personal memory box. Unfortunately all his treasures were dripping wet.

'Would you like me to take this and dry it out for you?' asked Maya.

Mister P flipped the lid of his suitcase closed and put his paw on the top. He rose heavily to his feet and Maya found herself face-to-face with the largest animal she had ever seen. She didn't dare move. She wished she hadn't touched the case. The bear came slowly towards her, forcing her to step back against the wall of the cave. Now she was stuck. There was nowhere to run and nowhere to hide. All she could do was wait

to see what would happen next. The bear pushed
his head forward and pressed his damp black
nose gently against Maya's. He closed his eyes
and breathed out. Maya relaxed a little. This felt
friendly, not aggressive. It was also completely
bananas. She tried to stifle a nervous giggle. The
bear stepped back and looked at her.

'Hello,' she said. 'Mister P? I'm Maya and
this is Granny Anne.'

Mister P turned to Gran and bowed.

'Goodness,' said Gran, bobbing
a small curtsy in return.

'I can't wait to tell Mum and Dad,' said Maya. 'I woke them last night. I knew I'd seen a boat. But they said my eyes were playing tricks on me. Now I've proved I was right and they were wrong.'

Gran looked flustered. She put her hands on Maya's shoulders. 'No! We mustn't tell anyone. We need to find out what the bear is doing here. If you tell your Dad he'll go and call in the Coastguard and have the bear carted off to the zoo. That would be **terrible**.'

At the mention of the word zoo, Mister P started to swing his head backwards and forwards, giving the impression that he was even less happy about the zoo idea than Gran.

'But wouldn't a Z-O-O'—Maya spelt out the word in case Mister P recognized it again—'know how to look after a polar bear better than us?'

'NO!' said Gran, louder this time. 'They'd put him in an enclosure for the rest of his life

and he'd never be able to run wild again. I
don't think Mister P is a z-o-o kind of bear.
You can tell by looking at him. If he was
supposed to be going to the z-o-o, he'd have it
written on his label, wouldn't he?'

Maya wasn't convinced by Gran's logic.
Maybe Gran was forgetting how dangerous
bears could be. It wasn't as if Mister P was a
pet she could take home and look after.

'Perhaps I could just tell Mum, then?'
suggested Maya.

'I don't think that would be a good idea
either,' said Gran. 'Apart from anything else,
we don't want to give her anything else to . . .'
Granny Anne paused as if choosing her words
carefully '. . . to worry about. She thinks I'm as
batty as a fruit bat already.'

'No she doesn't!' cried Maya.

Gran raised her eyebrows. 'I may not be
quite as sharp as I used to be, but I know what
your mum and dad are saying about me. I'm

not stupid and I'm not deaf.'

Maya sighed. 'But surely Mum and Dad will find out about Mister P. It's not going to be easy keeping him hidden.'

'We won't keep him secret forever,' said Gran. 'We'll just let him settle in and perhaps introduce him to a few people so he gets used to the idea. That way, by the time Mum and Dad get to meet him, he'll be far too friendly for them to fuss about.'

Maya didn't try to argue. Gran's mind was made up.

'So you PROMISE?' said Gran. 'Not a word to anyone.'

Maya nodded. 'OK. I promise.'

'You're a good girl. As long as we stick together, everything will be all right, you'll see.'

'You and me *and* Mister P?' Maya asked.

'Exactly that,' said Gran. 'You and me and Mister P!'

CHAPTER 5
SILENCE IS GOLDEN

Gran and Maya hurried along the beach. The tide was coming in and the sea was washing closer to their feet with each incoming wave. Maya knew Mister P would be safe in the back of the cave— the sea didn't reach that far—but she had been reluctant to leave him alone in the darkness.

Away from the bear, everything started to feel a bit unreal—almost as if she might have been dreaming after all. She was bursting to discuss Mister P with Mum and Dad, but she'd promised Gran so she knew she had to keep the secret locked inside her.

'You're late back,'
said Dad. 'I was about
to call the Coastguard.
Ring, ring.' Dad chuckled
and pulled his phone out
of his pocket and
pretended to answer it.
'Coastguard here.'

'Haha!' Maya rolled her eyes. It was one of
Dad's regular jokes—no one else found it very
funny.

'And how was Granny Anne today?' asked
Mum.

Maya hated the way Mum always asked this
question as if she was expecting bad news.

'Gran was fine—good—very well.'

'Really? Because Mrs Ross from next door
called me to say Gran had disappeared out and left
all the doors open in the pouring rain.'

'She'd just popped down to the beach,' said
Maya. 'There's no harm in that is there?'

Mrs Ross was always calling Mum about Granny Anne. Gran said Mrs Ross was a busybody and should mind her own business. Mum said it was very helpful having a next-door neighbour who could keep an eye on things.

'And what did the two of you get up to— causing trouble as usual, no doubt?' said Dad.

'Not at all,' said Maya. 'We . . . um . . . we collected some driftwood and we cleaned up all the plastic bags washed up by the storm.'

'Very good,' said Dad. 'At least Gran hasn't forgotten how to be an eco-warrior.'

Maya could feel the suitcase label almost burning into her hand inside her pocket. She didn't like lying, but what could she do? She ran upstairs before anyone could ask her any more questions.

Maya had to get through the rest of today and a whole night before she could go back to the cave. She pulled out the label and looked at it closely. Just holding it in her hand made her heart race with excitement. Maybe keeping Mister P secret was part of the fun. For certain the label was the most interesting thing she'd added to her memory box for a long time. She went to her table and cut out a piece of paper in the shape of a large bear.

Today I met a polar bear.
His name was Mister P.
He arrived here in a little boat
From far across the sea.
I suppose, in a funny way
he's a little bit like me!

She liked the way it sounded. She punched a hole in one corner and then looped Mister P's label through before hiding it in the bottom of her memory box. She sat in her window with her box on her lap and thought about the day. It was amazing what a storm could wash up onto a beach. Most things washed up by accident—but a polar bear with a suitcase saying *1 Lighthouse Cottages* didn't seem like an accident. In which case, what was he doing here?

CHAPTER 6
ANTS IN YOUR PANTS

Maya jiggled and wriggled at the breakfast table. She hadn't slept well. A mixture of thinking about the bear and worrying about her promise to Gran.

'Ants in your pants?' asked Dad. 'I'm not surprised, it's a beautiful day. I wish I could come with you to the beach and not have to spend the day at work.'

Maya tried to smile and concentrated on eating her toast. If Dad knew about the polar bear, he'd probably have ants in his pants too. It was a good thing Dad wasn't coming to the beach or things could get very complicated. Maya wondered if he would really send Mister P to a zoo. As soon as she'd finished she went to get ready.

Maya's canvas shoes were still wet from yesterday and the sand rubbed at her heels as she walked. Gran was waiting in her garden and together they went out of her back gate and hurried down to the beach and the cave. Mister P was lying in the entrance, licking at his fur. As soon as he saw them coming, he got to his feet.

Out in the daylight, for the first time, Maya could see the true size of the animal and he was even bigger than she remembered.

'Wow!' said Maya.

'Poor bear,' said Gran, as if she was talking about something perfectly normal. 'The first thing we need to do is get rid of all that sand, dirt, and seaweed from his fur and make him more comfortable. Let's take him to the boat shed for a freshwater bath.'

'Come on, Mister P,' called Maya. She ran along the beach, Mister P galloping behind her kicking up sand and Gran scurrying along at the back.

Granny Anne's boat shed had been in her family for generations. Gran always kept it locked but everyone in the family knew the code; it was the day and month of Granny Anne's birthday—23rd August—2 3 0 8. Maya waited as Gran fumbled with the padlock, fiddling with the dials to turn each one to the right number. Mister P watched with his head tipped to one side. Gran pulled at the lock angrily.

'It's not working,' she mumbled, then looked at Maya. 'You have a go!'

Before Maya had a chance to move, Mister P leapt forward, grabbed the padlock with his teeth, and started pulling for all he was worth. The door creaked and bulged on its rusty old hinges.

'Not YOU!' said Maya. 'ME! You'll pull the whole place down if you do that.'

Maya nudged him to one side. She frowned as she looked at the numbers Gran had put in. They were completely wrong. 'Have you decided to change your birthday, or something?' Maya asked playfully as she shifted the dials and the lock popped open.

Gran looked at her hands. 'My fingers must be getting old,' she mumbled.

Inside, the boat shed was clean and tidy and bright. Surfboards stood against the back wall alongside a rail of black wetsuits and life jackets. On one side was a long table covered in old fishing crates filled with snorkels, masks, buckets and spades, and beach games. This is where the fun started. This is why Maya's friends loved coming to the beach with Granny Anne.

'Buckets,' said Gran, handing Maya a large blue bucket. They filled the buckets at the outside tap then took it in turns pouring the water over Mister P. In spite of her size, Gran was strong and had no problem hurling buckets of water at the bear. Maya struggled and seemed to go at half speed of Gran.

Gran laughed and whooped. 'Water fight!' she shouted.

'Not fair,' shouted Maya as another bucket of water slopped over the top of Mister P and onto her head. Gran looked happier than Maya had seen her in ages.

Maya filled her last bucket, but hadn't got the energy to throw it.

'I win,' said Gran.

Mister P picked up Maya's bucket and emptied it straight over Gran's head.

Gran thought that was funnier than ever.

'You'll get used to Granny Anne,' Maya whispered. 'She's not like most grannies.'

'A problem shared is a problem halved,' said Gran.

'What's that supposed to mean?' said Maya.

'It means that dealing with an old granny like me should be easier with the help of Mister P.'

The cold from her wet clothes had started to eat into Maya's skin and she was shivering. She snuggled in close to the bear and wished she had his thick fur.

Gran's teeth were chattering too. 'Time for an emergency hot chocolate, I think,' said Gran. 'We'll take Mister P back to the cave. He should be comfortable now he's clean.'

Mister P didn't seem very keen to go back to the cave. Maya found three old towels and carried them to the cave, laying them out on some flat rocks for him to lie on. They sat with him for a few minutes to make sure he was

settled and Maya stroked his paw while Gran
sang him one of her songs from the sea. Her
singing voice was wobblier than it used to be,
but Mister P seemed to enjoy it and soon he was
snoring happily and didn't wake up, even when
Maya and Gran crept out.

CHAPTER 7
TAKE ONE DAY AT A TIME

Granny Anne and Maya walked back to the house in silence. They were too cold to talk. As soon as they were inside, they stripped off their wet clothes and Gran fetched a couple of old sweaters, all bobbly and full of holes, and gave one to Maya before pulling one over her own head. They stood in the kitchen.

'Now what was I going to do?' said Gran.

'Emergency hot chocolate?' said Maya. 'That's what you said.'

'Oh yes.' Gran stood with her hands on the kitchen top and stared at them. Maya waited. It was as if Gran couldn't work out where to start. 'Shall I get the milk?' asked Maya.

'Milk, yes, thank you.'

Gran got the mugs and chocolate down from the cupboard while Maya poured milk into a saucepan. They watched the milk carefully as it heated up then poured it into the mugs.

Gran took a gulp. 'That's better,' she said, sitting down at the table with a new packet of biscuits. Maya pulled up her knees under the sweater and felt the warmth of the chocolate in her tummy.

'Have you still got your marbles?' Maya asked. 'We haven't played for ages.'

'Of course I have,' said Gran. 'They're in the games chest next door, where they always live.'

'Dad said he thought you'd lost them, that's all.'

Granny Anne tapped her fingertips together. 'Is that what he said? Those very words? That I'd lost my marbles?'

'Something like that,' said Maya.

Gran gulped down the last of her chocolate and banged the mug down on the table. 'I'm afraid your Dad isn't talking about those glass marbles next door,' she said. 'When you say that someone is losing their marbles, it means that they are a bit forgetful or that their brain isn't working very well. It's not polite.'

Maya felt stupid and embarrassed and angry with Dad. 'I'm sorry,' she stuttered. 'I didn't mean . . .'

'Don't worry,' said Gran. 'You can tell your Dad that I've got plenty of marbles left. It'll take a little while longer before I lose them all.'

'It'll take *forever*,' said Maya.

'Let's hope so!' Gran picked up Maya's envelope. 'You left this here yesterday.'

'Oh yes—it's the invitation for your party.

I wanted to show it to you, to make sure it was OK.'

'I didn't know I was having a party,' said Gran. 'How lovely.'

'Haha,' said Maya. 'Very funny.'

Gran wasn't laughing. Maya fetched Gran's calendar off the wall and pointed to a square decorated with balloons. '23rd August: Gran's Beach Party.'

'23rd August? That's my birthday,' said Gran.

'Well exactly. So that is why we are having a party, remember?'

Gran rubbed her eyes and then read each line of the invitation aloud. 'It's a beautiful invitation, Maya. Thank you. I will look forward to it.'

Maya hung the calendar back on the wall. Gran tapped her fingers together.

'Do you know, if we're having a party down on the beach, perhaps we could invite Mister P? He'll add a bit of excitement.'

BANG!

Gran's door flew open and Mister P stood in the doorway.

'Oh my goodness!' cried Maya, leaping to her feet. 'What are you doing here? Quick, get inside before someone sees you.' She stood back and ushered him in through the door. 'How did you find us?'

'He must have heard us talking about him,' said Gran.

'He'd have to have pretty good hearing for that!'

Mister P stuck his nose in the air and sniffed.

'Or perhaps he has good smell!' said Gran.

'I think he is just nosy!'

Mister P sniffed some more. He sniffed across the table then stuck his nose into Maya's empty mug of chocolate. There was a strange bubbling sound as if he was trying to suck all the dregs out of the bottom. He lifted his head with the mug still stuck on the end of his snout. Maya did her best to keep a straight face. Mister P frowned in concentration as he tried to figure out what to do. First he gave his head a small shake.

'Careful, Mister P,' said Maya, trying to grab the mug.

Mister P shook his head again, more violently this time. Suddenly the mug popped off the end of his nose, flew across the room, and smashed against the wall.

'Oops!' said Maya, jumping out of the way.

Mister P gave his nose a rub and looked at the broken china spread across the floor.

'Oh dear! That was one of my favourite cups,' said Gran. 'It was one Grandpa Ted gave me.'

Mister P pushed a chocolatey nose in Gran's direction, as if to say sorry. Gran held up her hands. 'I'm sure you didn't mean to do it, Mister P, but I don't want all that polar bear chocolate dribble spray in my face, thank you very much. The best thing you can do is to stay out of the way or you're going slice your paws open on these sharp pieces of china.'

Gran could be quite fierce when she wanted and Mister P hung his head and watched out of the corner of his eyes as Gran swept into action with her dustpan and brush.

'Maybe we could use Dolphin's bowl for Mister P?' said Maya. 'It might be safer.'

'Dolphin's bowl?' said Gran, looking up from examining the floor to make sure she hadn't missed any splinters of china. 'But Dolphin is dead.'

'Sorry,' said Maya, awkwardly, 'I just thought that if you still had his bowl then we could use it to give Mister P food or drink—to save anything else getting broken.'

'Oh, I see what you mean. Yes, good idea. You'll probably find it in the garage.'

Gran waved her hand towards the garage door and Maya went to search. Maya felt bad. She shouldn't have mentioned Dolphin. Dolphin was Gran's old dog. He died last year and Gran had been sadder than sad. Mum reckoned that Gran hadn't been the same since Dolphin had gone. 'It hits you hard losing a dog when you are that age,' she said. Mum worried a lot like that.

Maya looked around. How was she supposed to find Dolphin's bowl amongst all the clutter? The garage had been Grandpa Ted's workshop and Gran hadn't touched a thing since he died. Maya had never met Grandpa Ted, but Gran's house was full of photos and Maya knew everything about him.

In the middle of the garage, covering half the floor, was Grandpa Ted's hang glider. It was all in bits and was more dust and cobwebs than anything else. Gran was trying to persuade Max to fix it up so she could have a go, but Max was busy at work and Dad said no way was Gran going hang gliding.

The door creaked on its hinges and Mister P's large head appeared.

'Careful in here,' said Maya.

Mister P gave the hang glider a quick inspection then edged his way past. He paused and sniffed, then went straight to a cupboard and flicked it open.

'You've found it,' said Maya. 'How did you do that?'

Mister P tapped his nose a couple of times with his paw. Maya picked up the bowl and laughed. 'Looks like dinner is waiting for you!' She tipped it towards the bear so he could see the dead spider lying in the bottom.

Mister P grabbed the bowl between his teeth and hurled it across the garage like a frisbee, then ran for the door.

'What is going on in there,' called Gran. 'Tell that polar bear to be careful amongst all Ted's things.'

'It's OK,' said Maya, poking her head round the door. 'I don't think polar bears like spiders, that's all!'

Maya washed out Dolphin's bowl and put it on the floor. Mister P licked at the empty bowl and gave Maya a hopeful look. 'I suppose he might be hungry,' said Maya.

'Well there's plenty of fish in the sea,' said Gran.

'Maybe catching them is a problem. Polar bears hunt from the ice, don't they? They don't just swim along like a shark! They wait on the ice and then pounce!'

'Oh,' said Gran. 'Well you know more about it than I do. I'll have to look into it.' Gran nodded thoughtfully at the bear. Then she picked up Maya's invitation again.

'Are we having a party?' she asked.

Maya and Mister P sat down and looked at her.

'Gran! Stop it. You *know* we are having a party, we've just been talking about it.'

'Have we? I thought we'd been talking about polar bears? You can't expect me to remember everything you know. I lead a busy life. Now get me my calendar.'

Maya showed Gran the box with the balloons . . . again.

'23rd August.' said Gran. 'Isn't that my birthday?'

'Yes Gran,' said Maya as patiently as she could. 'It is.'

'Well as long as it's written on here, I won't forget, will I?' said Gran, firmly.

'As long as you remember to look at your calendar,' Maya mumbled.

The clock on Gran's wall showed it was
nearly lunchtime.

'I'd better go,' said Maya. 'I'll take Mister P
back to the cave before I head home.'

'I think I'd like to keep him here,' said Gran.

Maya sighed. 'No Gran. If you keep him here
then everyone will know about him.'

Gran thought about this for a moment. 'Well
don't let that busybody Mrs Ross see him when
you leave.'

Maya checked front and back to make sure no
one was about. She should be able to slip out of

Gran's back gate and down to the beach without anyone seeing. She kept low to the ground and Mister P crept along behind her.

Before long she and Mister P were trotting down the path back to the beach. She thought about Gran's party and wondered why Gran had been so forgetful. Perhaps she was just having a bad day. Perhaps the water fight had frozen her brain cells.

* * *

'How was Gran?' asked Mum.

Maya bit her lip. 'Fine. Completely fine.'

'Not too forgetful?'

'No.'

'Not doing anything funny?'

'Well we did have a water fight. That was quite funny.'

'You will tell us, Maya, if you notice anything.'

'Don't worry, I will.'

CHAPTER 8
FISHING FOR TROUBLE

Life with Mister P settled into some kind of a routine. He seemed to be comfortable in his cave home and Gran seemed to enjoy going to visit him. 'It gives me a new purpose,' said Gran. 'Now that you're at school and all grown up and clever, there's not so much for me to do any more. I like to feel useful.'

'What are you talking about?' replied Maya. 'I don't know what I'd do if you weren't here to help me. I'm definitely not grown up and clever and you are most definitely useful.'

'Use it or lose it, that's what I say. The best way to keep going is to be busy. And Mister P has certainly given us plenty to think about.'

Gran never seemed to stop thinking about Mister P. For the last few days she had been determined that Mister P was starving. It was beginning to make her quite anxious.

Maya felt sure the bear was finding food from somewhere. He didn't look starving. However, convincing Gran was tricky and Gran was determined to make sure he was well fed.

'I'd like you to bring a couple of friends to the beach, tomorrow,' said Gran. 'I have a top-secret mission in mind.'

Gran's missions were usually loads of fun so Maya knew she wouldn't have any trouble finding friends to come and join in.

'Does this top-secret mission involve Mister P?' asked Maya.

Gran tapped the side of her nose with her finger. 'It wouldn't be top-secret if I told you that, would it?' she said.

'But what will I tell my friends?'

'Nothing,' said Gran. 'You leave that to me.'

* * *

Mum was in a right old fuss. She was worried about Gran having three children to look after and wondered if she could persuade Iris to come and help.

Maya didn't mention that it would be three children and one large polar bear. She was also one hundred per cent certain that if you had to choose someone to take on a mission with a polar bear, Iris would NOT be that person. Iris was all boyfriends and drama and drama and boyfriends.

'We don't need Iris,' said Maya. 'We'll be fine—it's not as though Gran will do anything **stupid.**'

'Morning,' said Iris shuffling her way into the kitchen in her dressing gown and staring at Maya. 'What's that about not needing me? You'll have to put up with me for a few more weeks before getting rid of me to university, I'm afraid.'

'That's not what I meant,' said Maya. 'We were just talking about Gran's mission.'

'So what is Gran up to now?' said Iris, pouring herself a glass of water.

'She is plotting and planning goodness only knows what,' said Mum, 'and I was wondering if you'd like to go to the beach with Maya and a couple of her friends, just to keep an eye on things.'

'Sorry,' said Iris. 'But I have the worst headache. I think I must be going down with something. Anyway, as Maya says, she doesn't need *me*.'

Maya wanted to sink into the floor. Sometimes Iris had a way of making her feel sad. She watched Iris swallow two pills before stomping back upstairs. Mum raised her eyes to the ceiling then passed Maya a bag with a packed lunch and a drink.

'Please take care,' said Mum. 'You don't have to do everything Gran suggests. Come back home if you are at all worried.'

'It's you that worries, not me,' said Maya and she rolled her swimming things in a towel and set off. She was looking forward to seeing Callum and Lucy and the three of them should be able to handle one of Gran's missions without too much trouble.

* * *

'What are we going to do,' asked Lucy as they hurried down the hill together. 'It all sounds very **mysterious.**'

Maya wasn't sure what to expect herself. 'Who knows? But I have a feeling that there might be a something quite unusual involved. Something no one else knows about.'

'**Cool,**' said Callum.

'**OOOOhhh,**' said Lucy, 'A proper Granny Anne adventure then.'

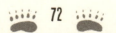

72

Gran met them outside the cave for a briefing. 'You need to understand that this mission is top-secret,' she said. 'You can only come if you promise to tell no one.'

Lucy and Callum nodded eagerly.

'In that case I think it is time to introduce you to the bear.'

Lucy and Callum laughed. 'The bear?' they said, looking at Maya.

At that moment, Mister P emerged from the darkness of the cave.

Callum and Lucy were speechless.

Gran put out her right hand and the others all had to put their right hands on top. Mister P added his paw for good measure.

'Repeat after me,' said Gran. 'I solemnly swear I will tell no one about the bear.'

Callum and Lucy repeated the words. Maya felt herself saying the words too, even though she wasn't sure she wanted to.

'Is that the mission, then?' asked Lucy. 'To

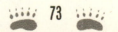

introduce us to the bear?'

'No!' said Gran. 'The mission is to take the bear on a trip to get food. But first we must prepare.'

They followed Gran back to the boat shed. Maya opened the lock before Gran had the chance to get it wrong again.

First Gran threw out life jackets. Maya, Callum, and Lucy looked at each other and then buckled them on. Unfortunately there was nothing big enough for Mister P, but Gran didn't seem too worried.

'Now you two take these,' said Gran handing an oar each to Callum and Lucy. 'Then I'll need your help to drag Mister P's boat to the water.'

'What?' said Maya. 'That old thing he arrived in?'

Gran was already striding along the beach. She'd tied the boat up way along the beach.

'The plan is to take Mister P fishing,' said Gran. 'I tried it on my own, last night, but I need more weight to stabilize the boat—which is where you three come in.'

'You went out by yourself last night?' said Maya. 'Gran, you shouldn't do that. It's not safe.'

'I had Mister P with me,' said Gran.

'And you think that makes it safer?' She noticed Mister P holding back which didn't fill her with confidence. 'Gran, are you sure this is sensible? There are quite a lot of us and it is a very small boat.'

'Yes, yes, it's fine,' said Gran, holding the boat steady as they clambered in. 'Don't you forget that I've spent all my life in boats.' She fixed the oars in place and then started to row.

With all the weight, the boat sat very low in the water and every now and again a wave sprayed over the edge, making them wet.

'Where are the fishing rods?' said Callum. 'We can't catch fish without a fishing rod.' Callum's dad was a fisherman, and his grandad too, so he was well used to fishing expeditions.

'We're fishing polar bear style,' said Gran. 'Paws only.' Mister P covered his face. Maya guessed that last night's expedition hadn't been a great success.

Gran passed the oars to Mister P and directed him towards a rocky point. She inspected the water carefully. 'This will do,' she said and dropped the small anchor over the side.

'Now,' she said, 'I need the three of you on *this* side of the boat.'

The boat tippled and topped as Maya,
Callum, and Lucy tried to shuffle themselves
into position along one side.

Gran waited for the boat to steady and then
picked up a snorkel and mask. She fixed the
mask over Mister P's nose and snapped the
elastic over the back of his head. The mask made
his face go all squishy and Callum and Lucy
giggled. Then Gran put the
snorkel tube into place.

'I still say it would be easier with a fishing rod,' said Callum.

Gran gave him a look. 'He is a polar bear. He doesn't fish with a rod. He uses his paws.'

'I don't think polar bears normally fish with snorkels and masks either,' said Lucy.

Gran frowned. 'It's different in the Arctic,' she said.

'And why use the boat?' Lucy continued. 'Wouldn't it be easier to fish off the rocks?'

Gran sighed a loud sigh. 'Do you want to help on this mission or not? And you should know never to fish off those rocks because there is always a danger of being cut off by the tide.'

Maya saw Lucy and Callum glance at each other. She felt bad. It was obvious that neither of them were enjoying this and nor was Mister P. But when Gran put her mind to something, nothing could stop her.

On Gran's instructions, Mister P leant over the side of the boat and put his face in the water.

The boat tipped dangerously to one side.

'Lean the other way, lean the other way,' shouted Callum. **'We're going to capsize.'**

Callum, Maya, and Lucy leant back as far as they could without falling out.

'This is mad,' said Lucy. 'How long have we got to stay like this.'

'My back is hurting,' said Callum.

'Stay quiet,' said Gran. 'Mister P needs to concentrate.'

Suddenly, with a splash, Mister P thrust his paw into the water and pulled out . . . a huge flubbery jellyfish. He looked at it in horror.

'Ahhhhh!' screeched Lucy.

'Put it back! Put it back!' cried Callum.

There was a lot of splashing and shouting as the boat rocked from side to side.

'Hold steady! Hold steady!' called Gran.

Mister P lobbed the jellyfish overboard and everyone relaxed.

'If at first you don't succeed, try, try, try again!' Gran said.

But Mister P refused to put his paws back into the water. He ripped off his mask and flung it into the bottom of the boat.

'Can we go back now?' asked Callum. 'This mission is silly.'

Lucy nodded.

'And the wind is getting up,' said Maya.

Gran looked disappointed. 'Very well,' she said. 'If that's how you all feel.'

Rowing back was hard. They were going against the breeze and the water was choppy. They took it in turns with the oars, but they were getting nowhere. Gran started getting rather confused. Water splashed over the sides and Callum did his best to bail it out with an old tin.

Finally Mister P took the oars again and things moved faster, but by the time they got back to the beach, everyone was wet and grumpy and exhausted. They sat on their towels and ate their picnics in silence. Maya gave Mister P half her sandwich and he chewed and swallowed the bread in a rather half-hearted way.

'If it's fresh fish you are after, why don't you go down to the harbour and get some from Grandad,' said Callum. 'It would be a lot easier and a lot safer.'

'I don't buy fish from people I don't know,' said Gran.

'But you *do* know Grandad,' said Callum. 'You've known him for years.'

'Have I?' said Gran.

'It's Ozzy,' said Maya. Ozzy was one of Gran's oldest friends.

Gran clapped her hands together. '**Ozzy!** Of course! Why on earth didn't I think of that? He'll have plenty of fish.'

'Is your Gran feeling all right?' whispered Callum.

Maya looked out at the sea. This trip had already been a bit embarrassing. It didn't help when Gran couldn't remember her best friend.

The tide was coming in fast. 'Why don't we play Last Man Standing?' suggested Maya.

Last Man Standing was one of Gran's favourite beach games. The idea was to build a big wall of sand to hold back the sea and stop it reaching your feet. The last one with dry feet was the winner.

'**On your marks . . .** get set **. . . GO!**' shouted Gran. Everyone started digging for all they were worth.

Mister P watched with interest before scooping up great pawfuls of sand to construct a wall of his own. He was a master digger and used his nose as well as his paws to push the sand into position. Soon his wall was higher and wider than anyone else's.

'Good work,' laughed Maya.

With each wave, the water came closer and closer. They squealed and shouted at the sea to '*go away*' as it lapped against their sand defences. First Callum's feet got wet, then Maya's, then Lucy's, and then Gran's. Mister P stood peering over the top of his huge wall.

'You win, Mister P,' they called. 'You are the last bear standing.'

Mister P refused to move. He watched and waited as bit by bit the sea ate away at the sand and his wall began to collapse. Finally a large wave rolled in. Mister P bared his teeth and growled as it approached. The others held their breath. The water crashed over the great mound of sand, leaving nothing but a small bump. Mister P sat down in a huff, staring at his four wet paws.

'Time and tide wait for no man,' said Maya, laughing.

'Or bear,' said Callum.

'The sea comes in and the sea goes out—twice a day, every day—and there's nothing any of us can do about it,' said Lucy.

Mister P stared at the next wave as it approached. He waited until it was almost at his feet and then bounded off up the beach towards his cave.

'He's funny,' said Callum.

'And clever,' said Lucy.

'Now remember your promise, all of you,' said Gran. 'It is very important that we tell no one about the bear. His life may depend upon it.' She wiggled her eyebrows up and down.

'We'll remember,' they said.

Maya looked at the bear standing in the mouth of his cave. She had a feeling it was going to be hard to keep him secret for much longer.

* * *

'How was Gran?' Mum asked, not even looking up.

'All right.'

'She didn't do anything unusual or stupid?'

'No.'

'Are you sure?' Dad asked the question carefully. 'It's just that I've had Lucy's mum on the phone. Apparently Gran took you on rather a *strange* fishing trip.' Dad emphasized the word *strange*.

Maya's cheeks went hot. What had Lucy said? 'We rowed out to the point. Dabbled around a bit, that's all. We had life jackets on.' Maya couldn't look at Dad. She wasn't exactly lying, but she wasn't exactly telling the truth either.

'And . . .'

'And nothing. Then we rowed back again.' Maya could tell Dad was fishing for trouble.

'But Gran hasn't got a boat any more. So how did you row out to the point?'

Maya thought fast. 'We found one on the beach.'

Dad tapped the tips of his fingers together. 'So Gran stole a boat from the beach and took you all out to the point and then tried to bring you back again against the tide.' Dad made it sound like half statement, half question and Maya wasn't sure if she needed to answer.

'Borrowed,' said Maya. 'She borrowed the boat.'

'From . . . ?'

'From Mister . . .' Maya had to stop herself quickly. 'From the beach,' said Maya.

'And the fishing rods?'

'We didn't need fishing rods. We were using our paws.'

'Really,' said Dad nodding his head up and down slowly. 'Your paws. Interesting. And you don't think there is anything strange about that?'

Maya looked at the floor. 'It was just a game.

One of Granny Anne's adventures.'

Dad leant forward and took Maya's hands. 'Please don't let Gran take you out fishing with your paws again.'

Gran's last fishing trip

CHAPTER 9
GOING DOWNHILL FAST

When Maya got to Gran's the next morning, Mister P had already made his way to the house and was waiting in the kitchen.

'What are you doing up here, Mister P? You can't just wander around when you feel like it. It doesn't work like that for a polar bear round here.'

Mister P looked hopefully into Dolphin's empty bowl.

Gran was rocking backwards and forwards, too fast, in her rocking chair. She seemed anxious. Maya hoped she hadn't been out fishing again during the night.

'I don't think Mister P has had breakfast,' said Gran. 'What are we going to do?'

'Why don't we go down to the harbour and get some fish, like Callum suggested,' said Maya.

'That's a good idea. Who's Callum?'

'You know—Callum! Callum who was with us yesterday. Ozzy's Callum.'

'Ozzy!' exclaimed Gran. 'Now why didn't I think of him before. He's bound to have some spare fish on board his boat.'

Maya was starting to get confused herself. Gran pulled on her sandals. 'We'll take Mister P with us,' she said.

Maya laughed. 'Don't you think people might notice if we turn up with a polar bear?'

'Well, I'm certainly not leaving him in the house. Who knows what damage he might do. And I'd like to introduce him to Ozzy.'

'If we are going to introduce him to Ozzy, couldn't we introduce him to Mum and Dad too? It would make life much easier.'

Granny Anne picked up her basket. When she stood up, Maya could see tears in her eyes. 'Oh, please no,' she said. 'I don't want to lose Mister P. If your Mum and Dad find out about him, they'll either have *him* taken away or *me* taken away—*or both.* I'm not ready for that. Not yet.'

Maya didn't want to see anyone taken away.

Gran gave a loud sniff and wiped her sleeve across her eyes. Maya hated to see Gran upset. Gran's face was made for smiling, not crying and Maya decided she wouldn't mention telling her parents about Mister P again.

The road down to the port was steep. Gran danced down, her skinny legs poking out of her shorts. Mister P tried to dance down after her, but the surface was damp, slippery, and uneven, and his huge polar bear paws didn't want to behave.

Every now and again, Gran looked back

over her shoulder and grinned. 'Keep up, keep up,' she said. Mister P was doing his best, but as he picked up speed, Maya could see PANIC written all over his face. He tried to put on the brakes by lowering his backside onto the road, straightening his front legs against the slope, and trying to dig his claws into the hard surface, but his paws skidded out wildly in front of him and he ended up going head over heels, somehow landing back on his feet again.

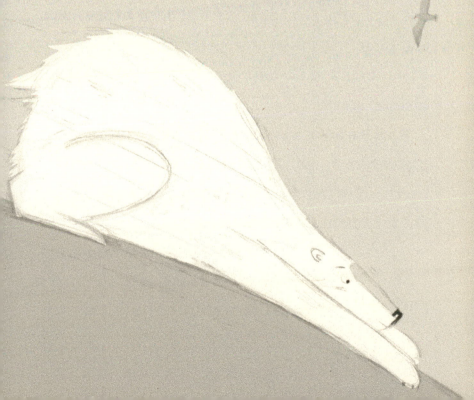

The sight of Gran pursued by a not-very-acrobatic polar bear was funny and Maya trotted behind laughing so much that tears streamed down her face. By the time they reached the bottom of the hill, poor Mister P's tongue was lolling out the side of his mouth and his chest was heaving with exhaustion. Gran patted him on the head.

The harbour was one of Gran's favourite places. She felt at home down amongst the fishing boats. Grandpa Ted had been a fisherman and Gran was full of stories about his fishing adventures and his daring rescues as part of the lifeboat crew.

The harbour was one of Maya's favourite places too. Seagulls shrieked and circled overhead or perched on the port walls and seats. Boats came and went, unloading their catch and laying out their salt-crusted fishing nets tangled with ropes and seaweed. She hadn't always liked it. When she first arrived, the smell of sea and salt and engine oil made her uncomfortable. Now she was used to it. It never changed. It was always there. It had the smell of belonging.

Mister P quickly recovered from his helter-skelter down the road. His button-black eyes took in the scene around him and his nose twitched as he took three deep bear breaths, closing his eyes as he inhaled. His stomach rumbled.

There weren't that many boats in that morning and Gran scanned the harbour before spotting Ozzy and raising her hand in an enthusiastic wave. '*There's* young Ozzy,' she said.

Maya giggled. Ozzy was about 85—even older than Gran. As they neared his old blue fishing boat, Ozzy leapt onto the jetty, giving Gran a big hug. Then he turned to Maya and gave her a hug too. 'Good morning ladies.

Callum said you might be coming. And who's this you've brought to see me today?'

Mister P opened his arms and squeezed Ozzy in a massive bear hug.

'**Ooooh, not too hard.** You'll be breaking all my ribs.'

Maya gently pulled Mister P's paws away and poor Ozzy took a few moments to get his breath back. 'Well!' he said, looking a little dazed. 'Where did you find this one?'

Granny Anne looked at Maya. 'Where did we find him?'

'We discovered him down at Home Beach, in the cave along from Granny Anne's boat shed,' said Maya. 'I thought I'd spotted a small boat out at sea a few nights ago and it turns out it was HIM.'

'Hmmm,' said Ozzy, stroking his beard thoughtfully. 'I don't suppose he'd have anything to do with the *strange* fishing trip you took my grandson on?'

Gran looked at her feet. 'What fishing trip?' she asked.

'Talking of fish,' said Maya, changing the subject. 'Have you got any spare? Anything that a polar bear might like?'

Mister P was busy examining one of Ozzy's fishing nets, pawing through the fine netting, and licking at it with his rough, dark tongue.

'He won't be getting anything if he starts ripping my nets. Tell that Mister B of yours that he needs to take care.'

'Mister *P*,' said Gran. 'His name is Mister P.'

'Well whatever he's called, I don't need him wrecking my gear or there'll be trouble.' Ozzy hopped back on board opened a hatch in the deck of the boat. 'Here, I can let you have a few of these. They are icy cold so just right for a polar bear, I would imagine.'

He threw a fish in Mister P's direction and Mister P tried to raise his paws in the air to catch it. Unfortunately they were tangled up in the netting and as the fish sailed over his head, Mister P fell backwards, opened his mouth, and caught the fish neatly between his teeth.

'Good save!' said Ozzy, laughing. He held out a second fish towards Maya. 'Here—dangle this over the bear's nose and do what you can to keep him occupied while I try to rescue my net.'

Distracting a polar bear was not something Maya had ever tried before. She dangled the fish just out of reach above his nose and Mister P lay quite still on his back, his nose following from side to side as he watched the fish swinging like a pendulum.

'You're feeling very sleepy,' said Maya, pretending to hypnotize the bear. 'After a count of ten you will do whatever I tell you.'

'In your dreams,' laughed Ozzy. 'That bear doesn't look remotely sleepy to me and he doesn't look much like one to obey orders either.'

Ozzy was right. Mister P was wide awake and didn't once take his eyes off the fish. In the meantime, Gran and Ozzy worked carefully to remove the net from around his claws. 'It looks like he's made a few holes,' said Ozzy, shaking his head.

'Oh, don't fuss,' said Gran. 'There's nothing too much to worry about here. I can pop back later and mend them. A stitch in time saves nine, that's what I always used to say to Ted. Sort these things out quickly and it'll save you lots of work later on.'

'You're the expert,' said Ozzy.

Finally, the net was free and Mister P continued to lie on his back, flexing and stretching his newly-released claws. Maya dropped the fish into his mouth. He crunched it, swallowed it, then sat up, patted his tummy, looked at Ozzy, and gave him what looked like a salute.

Ozzy chuckled and saluted back.

'You've got a right one there, Anne,' he said. 'Will he be sticking around for long?'

'Only as long as he needs to,' said Gran.

'Right,' said Ozzy, grinning. 'Well that's clear as day then.'

Ozzy filled Gran's basket with more fish. 'That should keep you going for the time being. I'll try to keep some of our catch on one side for you. No promises, though. The moon isn't right at the moment.'

Ozzy said goodbye to Gran, but held Maya back. 'How is your Gran,' he said. 'She doesn't seem quite herself. It sounds like she gave you all a bit of a fright with that fishing trip of hers.'

'It's been hard for her—trying to take care of a polar bear,' said Maya.

'You look after her then,' said Ozzy. 'She's a special lady.'

'I'm doing my best,' said Maya.

With a full tummy, and with the sun heating

up, Mister P huffed and puffed his way back up the steep hill towards Gran's house, his steps getting slower and slower, his grumbles getting louder and louder. Maya tried to help by pushing him from behind, but it was like pushing a small car. When they got back to Gran's kitchen, Mister P flopped down on the floor.

'What's Dolphin's bowl doing there?' said Gran, pointing at the floor.

Maya swallowed and took her time. 'We're using it for Mister P—*remember?*'

Gran bent down and picked up the bowl and held it close to her. 'But Dolphin is dead.' A silence filled the kitchen and Maya didn't know what to say. Granny Anne stared long and hard at Mister P. Then rubbed her eyes as if she was very tired.

'I do miss Dolphin,' she said.

CHAPTER 10
FACING THE MUSIC

A week went by and nothing too odd happened. Every morning Maya and Gran would go to the harbour to pick up fish and then take them down to the beach for Mister P. Sometimes Callum or Lucy came with them. Gran and Maya introduced Mister P to the rock pools and the snappy crabs who lived in them, to the distant pods of dolphins who sometimes played in the bay, and to the skills of building giant sandcastles. With Mister P to help them dig, the sandcastles got bigger and bigger and more and more elaborate. Gran was happy in the company

of Mister P and her brain seemed less forgetful when he was around.

Mister P seemed to be happy too and he was beginning to find his way around—which was giving rise to a few problems.

'You can't just wander up the path and visit Gran whenever you want,' said Maya, sternly. 'If Mrs Ross spots you then she'll tell Mum and Dad straight away and you'll get all of us into trouble.'

'And you can't go foraging for fish down at the port either,' said Callum, 'or Grandad says he's going to get in trouble too.'

Lucy suggested moving Mister P to the boat shed which everyone thought was a good idea. 'He'll be safer in there and at least you'll know where he is.'

So on Friday afternoon, Maya left Mister P in the boat shed with his suitcase and a large bucket of fish. She wandered home in the warm sunshine and found Mum slumped in an armchair with a cup of tea in her hand and Dad sitting at the table thumbing through a climbing magazine. They both looked done in. The sound of Iris's music coming from upstairs was so loud it was almost making waves on the surface of Mum's tea.

'How was Granny Anne?' said Mum.

'Gran was very well, actually,' said Maya, pleased to be telling the truth. 'Busy.'

'Busy telling stories about polar bears,' said Dad without looking up from his magazine.

Maya's heart nearly stopped. 'What do you mean?'

'This is what happens when you put something in Gran's head,' said Dad. 'I expect you told her about that boat you thought you saw the other night. Something in a big white coat. And now, out of nowhere, Gran thinks she's walking around with a polar bear by her side, gathering food for him, and fishing polar bear style.'

'But I *didn't* say anything,' said Maya.

Dad closed his magazine and threw it onto the floor. 'So where's this wild idea of hers come from then?'

Maya thought for a moment then looked him in the eye. 'What if there IS a polar bear?'

'Oh, come on Maya. We all know there's not a polar bear. I know how much you love Granny Anne, but going along with Gran's stories isn't going to help her or anyone else. We have to face facts and this whole polar bear thing is just another sign that she is going downhill fast.'

Mum gave Dad an angry look. 'We said we wouldn't discuss this now.'

'Gran does everything fast,' said Maya. 'No one can keep up with her. You need to leave her alone and stop worrying.'

Dad stood up and pulled Maya into a gentle hug. 'You're right, physically she is in great shape—she's probably fitter than I am. It's her *mind* we're worried about.'

'Her marbles, you mean?' said Maya. She couldn't keep the anger out of her voice.

Mum raised her eyebrows and looked at Dad.

'I shouldn't have said that about losing her marbles,' Dad said. 'It wasn't kind and I don't want to hear you saying it either.'

'Gran had to explain what you meant. I thought when you said Gran was losing her marbles you meant like ACTUALLY losing her real marbles. Anyway now I DO understand because Gran explained and I DON'T agree.'

Mum held up both hands. 'Don't get cross. We're only trying to look out for her and you should be pleased we are worried. It shows we care.'

'I care too, but so what if she forgets something every now and again? So what if she's found a polar bear? What difference does it make?'

'It makes a difference because it's getting worse,' said Dad. 'We can't have her putting herself or anyone else in danger.'

'But Gran would never do that,' said Maya. 'Or not on purpose.'

'Exactly' said Dad. 'I agree that she'd never do it *on purpose*, but the time may come when she has to face the music and realize that her decisions aren't always as sensible as they should be. We all need to start thinking about the future.'

Maya felt as if the air had been sucked out of the room. She'd taught herself not to think too hard about the future. She liked things just as they were.

The noise of Iris's music echoed through the floorboards with a loud boom, boom, boom. Suddenly Mum flung open the door and yelled up the stairs, **'Iris, how many times do I have to tell you to turn the volume down?'**

Maya put her hands over her ears. She hated it when Mum shouted. It pulled at some memory deep inside her and made her scared. She was glad to see Max skidding into the kitchen.

'What's up?' he said, messing Maya's hair. Maya ducked out of the way. Max's curly dark hair was pulled back into a ponytail and he was wearing his wetsuit and a pair of flip-flops.

'Granny Anne is what's up,' said Dad. 'And her pet polar bear.'

'Oh, that!' Max grinned. 'He's the talk of the town is Gran's polar bear.'

Maya felt torn in half. She hated the way the whole family was making fun of Granny Anne and Mister P—it wasn't fair because Gran was right and they were wrong. But how could she tell them when she had *promised* Granny Anne not to say anything?

'Well I'm going surfing if anyone wants to come,' said Max. 'I'll be back in time for tea.'

Maya was on her feet straight away. Her mind was racing. If Max was off surfing, that would mean he'd be going down to Home Beach.

And he couldn't surf without his surfboard.

And his surfboard was in the boat shed.

And in the boat shed was . . .

MISTER P!

'I'm coming,' said Maya.

'Wait for me.'

CHAPTER 11
GETTING INTO DEEP WATER

You could tell Max was related to Gran just by looking at him. He had the same wiry legs and he went everywhere fast. Granny Anne had tried to persuade him to become a fisherman, like Grandpa Ted, but Max had other ideas and now he was an apprentice glassblower at a big glassworks.

Max took Maya's hand as they walked past Gran's cottage towards the steep path down to the beach.

'Are you OK, sis?' he asked.

'Kind of,' Maya replied. She loved it when he

called her 'sis'. Everyone at school was jealous that Maya had Max for a brother because he was so cool. If Maya could have chosen a brother, Max would have been it.

'You mustn't worry if Mum and Dad get upset. Parents do that sometimes. Mum is very stressed about Granny Anne and I think this polar bear thing is doing Dad's head in.'

Maya pulled on Max's hand and stopped. 'About this polar bear *thing*,' said Maya. 'The thing is . . . it isn't a *thing*. There really *is* a polar bear. Gran isn't making it up or imagining it. His name is Mister P and he's living in the boat shed.' Max burst out laughing and Maya stood facing him, her arms crossed.

'Honestly, you're worse than Gran sometimes,' said Max.

'Suit yourself,' said Maya. 'It's up to you whether you believe me or not. Ozzy knows. Callum and Lucy too.'

'Ah, so you're all part of Gran's great

conspiracy?' Max was trying to keep a straight face, but Maya could see more laughter twitching at the edge of his mouth. 'I'll race you down there and we'll see, shall we?'

'Fine, but don't say I didn't warn you.' Maya hurtled off down the path and Max pulled off his flip-flops and pounded down behind her. Within a few minutes they were outside the boat shed and Maya was breathlessly undoing the padlock. Even from the outside the smell of animal was unmistakable.

'Are you ready?' she asked. She flung open the doors and Max's legs crumpled beneath him. He fell to his knees on the sand, his mouth open, and his eyes wide. He stared at Mister P. Mister P stared back.

'Well?' said Maya.

Max nodded. 'Yes.' He nodded some more. 'Yes, there is a polar bear . . . in the shed. Wow! I didn't see that coming.'

'Mister P, meet my brother, Max. Sorry he

looks so shocked but he didn't believe you were real. It's his own fault for not listening to me.'

Maya zipped herself into her wetsuit and picked up her small bodyboard. 'Come on Mister P. Time for a swim. Last one in the water is a sissy.'

At that Max came to his senses. He leapt to his feet, grabbed his surfboard, and sprinted down the sand after Maya and Mister P.

'Stay to the left,' Max shouted at them. 'The rip current is strong at the moment and we need to stay well to the left or we'll get pulled way out to sea.'

'I know, stupid,' shouted Maya as she ran. 'Granny Anne has hammered that into my head about a hundred times.'

They splashed into the water, Maya and Max gasping with cold. Mister P beat them by a mile, pounding his way out through the waves as if they were made of air, leaping the white crests of water with legs out at full stretch then ducking and diving under the larger waves. In the water his fur looked sleek and smooth. Once they reached the deeper, darker water, Maya floated on her back and Mister P swam slowly backwards and forwards, nose in the air, making a gentle deep humming noise.

'You like this, don't you?' said Maya. She envied Mister P being so comfortable in the water. It had taken her ages to get over her fear and to learn to swim, but she had got there in the end, thanks to Gran.

Mister P closed his eyes and rolled over onto his back next to her.

'There are some good waves coming,' shouted Max. 'Get ready.'

They let another couple of smaller waves go past.

'This is the one!' Max started paddling for all he was worth. Maya and Mister P did the same.

The wave was bigger than Maya expected. She mistimed it and it flipped her off her board, sending her tumbling over and over. Salt water filled her nostrils and her mouth as everything became a mass of chaos and confusion. It was like spending a few seconds in a washing machine before she surfaced and all was clear again. She staggered out of the water and Mister P sat beside her on the beach.

'You all right?' shouted Max.

Maya coughed. 'Made a mess of that one,' she spluttered and watched as Max waded back out. The waves were getting more powerful and Maya wasn't that keen to keep going. She dried herself quickly and pulled on her leggings and a sweater.

'Hello,' said a sing-song voice behind her. 'Glad to see you are introducing Mister P to surfing.'

'Gran!' said Maya, trying to keep the surprise out of her voice. 'What are you doing down here?' Gran was wearing her battered old wetsuit and had her surfboard under her arm; a surprise as Maya hadn't seen Gran surfing in ages.

'I spotted you walking past the house with a strange man so I thought I'd better come and check up on you,' said Gran, pointing in Max's direction.

'That's not a strange man,' said Maya. 'It's Max!'

'Max? Is it really? Goodness he's grown.'

Maya laughed.

Max held up a hand and waved. Gran waved back and starting walking along the beach.

Maya turned onto her tummy, picked up a handful of sand, and let it trickle through her fingers. Max was 22. Gran had known him since he was born and he definitely wasn't still growing. And Gran had only seen him a few days ago—a week at most. She could understand Gran forgetting who Callum was but not recognizing Max? Her own grandson? That wasn't good. Maya shook her head. She could still feel water rattling around in her ears and it was annoying her. She tipped her head to one side and banged the opposite ear. When that didn't work, she stood up and did a handstand. That usually did the trick.

'Sometimes, Mister P,' said Maya as she walked a few steps along the beach on her hands, 'sometimes I wonder if Gran's head turns upside down for a few seconds then flips back the right way again.' She dropped her feet back to the ground.

Mister P tipped his head to one side, banged his ear then buried his front paws in the sand and tried to kick up his back legs. Maya laughed as she watched him. He toppled first one way and then the other. She did her best to help him get his balance, but he was far too heavy for her to hold.

'You're nearly there, Mister P. One more try!'

Mister P kicked up again and managed to balance for a couple of seconds, his teeth gritted, his front legs quivering with effort, and his fur hanging in all the wrong direction. Then he collapsed in a heap on the sand.

Maya was doubled over with laughter. She looked around to see if the others were watching and spotted Max paddling for the next wave. But where was Gran?

'Ohhhh no!' she said out loud. 'Granny Anne!' Maya screamed at the top of her voice and started running down the beach. 'Don't go in there! It's too close to the rip! Come back!'

Maya's words were dragged away by the

wind. She watched helplessly as Gran paddled slowly towards the deeper water at the most dangerous point on the beach.

By now Max had spotted her too. **'Gran!'** he yelled, waving both arms in the air. **'GRAN! STOP!'**

He tried to get across to Gran, but it was too late, Gran was already getting into deep water and before Max could reach her, she was being sucked out to sea. Maya tried to control the panic and think clearly about what Dad had taught her. She knew the worst thing to do was to try to rescue Gran. That would end up with two people being in trouble instead of one. She could see Gran trying to swim sideways out of the current, but it was too strong for her and she was being taken further and further out.

Mister P was on his feet and splashing out through the breaking waves. It seemed as if he understood what he needed to do. He didn't try to battle the current, he just let it drag him out, swimming with it, not against it. The bear moved fast, powering his way towards the tiny shape of Granny Anne. He was the strongest swimmer that Maya had ever seen. Max had come out of the water and joined Maya and now they clung to each other as they watched Gran and Mister P appearing and disappearing in the waves.

'He will save her, won't he?' squeaked Maya. She was shivering violently.

'Polar bears can swim hundreds of miles,' said Max. 'If anyone can save Granny Anne, it's Mister P.'

The bear swam closer and closer and soon he was up level with Granny Anne. They were so far out, they were just a white blob and a black dot in the sea. 'It's getting rougher,' Maya whispered.

Max nodded and held on to her a little tighter. Fear prickled at Maya's chest. Memories. She buried her face against Max's wetsuit.

'Look! I think he's got her,' said Max.

Maya allowed herself to peep. Gran was

hanging on to Mister P's back and he was swimming, swimming, swimming, taking a slow, diagonal line out towards safer water.

'He's doing the right thing,' said Max.

Maya tried to nod but her neck was rigid and her head heavy. It seemed to take forever until Mister P was back in the safe zone. Only then did he begin to make his way towards the shore, Granny Anne holding on for dear life.

Maya gulped in some deep breaths and Max loosened his hold on her.

'I thought she was going to drown,' sobbed Maya. 'And I don't know what I'd do if anything happened to her.'

'She's going to be all right,' said Max, crouching down, with his hands on Maya's arms. 'Do you hear me, Maya? Granny Anne is going to be OK.'

Maya nodded. She wanted to see Gran safe back on the beach.

'Now go and get the towels,' said Max. 'Gran might be in shock and we'll need to keep her warm.'

Maya was pleased to have something to do and by the time she'd got back, Max and Mister P were bringing Gran out of the water. They sat her gently on the beach and wrapped her in the towels. She was very pale and breathless and Maya held her hand and gave it a squeeze while Max took her pulse.

'I'm all right,' she said hoarsely.

Max raised his eyebrows. 'You're lucky to be

alive,' he said. 'What did you think you were doing?'

The colour was beginning to come back into Gran's cheeks, but her eyes remained dull. 'I thought it was . . . the other way.'

'The rip?' said Max.

'I see my mistake now,' she said. 'I don't know why I got so confused.'

'Don't worry about it. The important thing is that you are safe,' said Max. 'I think we should get you home.'

Gran's legs were too wobbly to stand, let alone walk, but Mister P was happy to help. He lay down and let Gran clamber onto his back before starting the slow journey back to Home Cottage. By the time they reached Gran's door, she was looking more lively. 'I think I can manage by myself now,' she said, sliding off Mister P's back and landing on her feet.

'I'm not so sure about that,' muttered Max.

CHAPTER 12
OUT OF SIGHT, OUT OF MIND

They ran Gran a hot bath and went to sit in the kitchen. Mister P was restless and seemed slightly shocked as well. Maya went to Gran's fridge and found him some of Ozzy's sardines.

'That had to be the worst moment of my life,' said Max. 'I can't believe what Gran did! We could so easily have lost her. I honestly don't know what we would have done if Mister P hadn't been there. I'm not sure I would have been strong enough to get Gran out of that current.'

At the sound of his name, Mister P looked up from his bowl and grinned.

'I hate to think what Mum and Dad are going to say about this.'

'About what? Gran nearly drowning or Gran hanging out with a polar bear?'

'BOTH!' said Max.

'Well let's not tell them then. They worry too much as it is and Gran is OK now.'

'Gran is NOT OK, Maya. We *have* to tell them. Imagine if we hadn't been there today when Gran went surfing! Imagine if we'd had to try and rescue Gran ourselves and the rip was too powerful. We might have drowned too. This is serious. You can't sweep this whole thing under the carpet and pretend it didn't happen. Mum and Dad need to know. They need to know *everything*.'

'But Gran made me promise not to tell them about Mister P. She says Dad will have him carted off to a zoo and then I would never forgive myself after everything he has done to help. I think Mister P is keeping Gran going. She loves that bear. Can we keep quiet about him for a bit longer—just for Gran?'

Mister P tipped his head on one side and gazed at Max with his big black eyes.

Max covered his face with his hands. 'OK. OK! What can I say when I've got a polar bear looking at me like that? But if Mum and Dad find out, you do realize we'll be in deep trouble. All of us.'

Maya nodded.

* * *

It was a while before Gran made it back into the kitchen. She'd put on her pyjamas and a warm jacket, and her long hair was dripping down her back.

'Hello,' she said looking at Max and sounding surprised. 'What are you doing here?'

Max stared at her in amazement.

'He's here to help,' said Maya.

'Help with what?' said Gran, looking around.

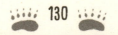

'I don't need help.'

Max raised his eyes to the ceiling. 'Never mind,' he said. 'I think I'll take Mister P to the garage and leave you two to chat.'

'Show Mister P the hang glider,' said Gran. 'You're supposed to be fixing that up for me, remember?'

'Yes Gran. I remember. It's not *me* that has the memory problem.'

'Goodness, Max has grown,' said Gran as Max and Mister P left the room. 'And he's quite cheeky nowadays.'

Maya made Gran a cup of tea and tucked a blanket round her. Max and Mister P were making a terrible noise in the garage, but Gran was so tired that it wasn't long before her eyes closed and she fell asleep. Maya watched her for a while then tiptoed towards the garage and put her head round the door. Max and Mister P were both wearing protective masks and Max had some weird tool in his hand that sent bright yellow sparks everywhere when it touched the metal.

Maya covered her ears and Max stopped, raising the cover from his face.

'Gran's asleep,' said Maya, closing the door.

'Thank goodness for that. Honestly, sometimes I wonder if she even knows who I am.'

'She says you've grown,' said Maya. 'She never tells me I've grown.'

Max flipped the cover down and continued welding the metal of the hang glider. Maya had to wait until his next stop before she could speak again.

'Is it nearly finished?' she said, walking slowly round the huge frame.

'It's beginning to take shape,' said Max. 'Pass me the screwdriver please, Mister P.' Mister P had a fistful of tools and stuck out his paw for Max to take what he needed.

'Gran knows who *you* are,' said Max. 'She

doesn't ask what *you* are doing here.'

Maya could see the hurt on Max's face and could hear the sadness in his voice. It made her feel guilty. Max had been part of Gran's life for way longer than Maya.

'I see more of her than you do, that's all it is,' Maya said.

'Out of sight, out of mind. Is that what you mean?'

'Kind of,' said Maya. 'She'll be fine when she wakes up. You'll see.'

Max shook his head and tightened a screw. 'I don't know why I'm even bothering to fix this thing up. Gran is never going to use it.'

His phone buzzed and he pulled off his head gear and fumbled in his pocket.

'It's Mum, wondering where we are,' he said, reading the text and checking the time. 'We should get back, I suppose.'

'Do you think it's all right to leave Gran by herself?' asked Maya.

'We'll leave Mister P with her. He's rescued her once so I'm sure he can keep an eye out.'

'I hope Mrs Ross doesn't call round.'

Max put his arm around Maya and laughed. 'If Mrs Ross bumped into a polar bear, it might cure her of being so nosy!'

He took the protective mask off Mister P and closed the lid of the tool box. 'Look after Granny Anne,' he said to the bear. 'And stay out of trouble.'

Maya gave Mister P a quick hug. The bear stood at the door and watched them leave.

'Things are getting a lot

worse with Granny Anne,' said Max as they walked up the hill towards the lighthouse. 'I think Dad may have a point. Perhaps we do have to start thinking about Gran's future.'

'She'll be better in the morning, when her brain isn't tired,' said Maya.

'We'll need to change the lock on her boat shed to make sure she doesn't go surfing again.'

'There's no need,' said Maya. 'She can't remember the code number anyway.'

Gran's last time on a surfboard

CHAPTER 13
THE LAST STRAW

They sat around the kitchen table. Mum, Dad, Max, Iris, and Maya. They'd finished eating and cleared the plates. Iris was painting her long nails with shiny blue nail varnish and Dad was tapping the end of his fork up and down. Usually Maya enjoyed all the chatter around the table, but not tonight.

'Gran got caught in the rip! Honestly?' said Dad.

Max nodded.

Dad put his hands flat on the table. 'This is the last straw! You know how dangerous that rip

can be? You could have died—all three of you.'

'But we're all OK,' said Maya.

'Except, clearly, my mother isn't safe to be left alone any more,' said Mum.

'Granny Anne isn't alone,' said Maya. 'She's got all of *us*.'

'But we can't be with her 24 hours a day.' Mum walked to the window and looked out. 'I mean, what if she suddenly wanders off and gets lost. The coast is dangerous enough at the best of times. I'd never forgive myself if anything happened.'

'But she won't wander off and get lost,' said Maya. 'She knows every street, every path, every brick of every house.'

Everyone turned to look at Maya. It was that look that told her to shut her mouth and that they all knew better than she did. Sometimes Maya still felt like the odd one out—as if she didn't quite belong. She stood awkwardly, wishing the moment would pass. They were

wrong about Gran. Wrong, **wrong**, **wrong**.
Weren't they?

'Gran only got muddled for one tiny moment,' Maya said, quietly. 'She hasn't been surfing in ages and she forgot.'

'Forgot?' The word burst out of Dad. 'Granny Anne was pretty much born on that beach. She's taught everybody in this family about water safety. She was a volunteer rescue officer for the Coastguard for about forty years. You don't FORGET, Maya.'

Maya wanted to cry. She'd like to forget this whole incident had ever happened.

Mum sat down again. 'Perhaps we should bring Granny Anne here to live with us.'

Iris put down her nail varnish and stared at Mum. 'Are you joking? Where would she sleep? She's not having *my* room.'

'But you're off to uni,' said Max.

'I know, but it's still MY room.'

'Gran would never want to move here,' said

Maya. 'She loves Home Cottage. She's happy there. She's lived there all her life.' There was a long silence.

'Anyway,' said Dad. 'I'm sorry, I'm going to have to go. I'm on night shift.'

Mum sighed. 'I think I'd better go down to Home Cottage and check Gran is all right.' She looked at Dad. 'Can you drop me on your way?'

Maya and Max looked at each other. If Mum and Dad went to Home Cottage now they would see more than just Gran. They'd discover Mister P too. And that could only make things worse.

'You don't need to go, Mum,' said Maya. 'Gran is fine, isn't she Max?'

Max didn't reply.

'I'm sorry, Maya' said Mum. 'I don't like to leave you, but Max and Iris are here to look after you. Gran is my mother and I am responsible for her. I won't be able to sleep unless I go and check on her. I won't be long.'

Iris finished her nails and held up her hands in front of her face. 'Perfect,' she said. 'I'm afraid I won't be here this evening. I've got a date with Sam. I'd better go and get ready.' Sam was Iris's new boyfriend and Iris hadn't talked about much else for the last week.

'You're out with Sam again?' asked Mum. 'Well don't be too late. I don't need anything else to worry about.'

Mum put on her coat and followed Dad out of the door. Maya paced round and round the kitchen. 'Don't just sit there Max. DO something.'

Max spread his hands.

'You're useless,' said Maya. She grabbed the phone and punched in Gran's number.

Brrrrr,
        brrrrr . . .

A lot of the time Gran didn't answer . . .

Brrrr, brrrr . . .
                Brrr, brrr . . .

On the sixth ring Gran picked up. 'Gran! Gran! It's Maya. Mum and Dad are on their way. You need to do something about Mister P.'

Granny Anne sounded as though she'd only just woken up. 'Hello? Who's that? Who? Do what?'

Maya tipped her head back.

'GRAN! PLEASE LISTEN TO ME. YOU HAVE TO GET MISTER P OUT OF THE HOUSE. QUICKLY. BEFORE MUM AND DAD GET THERE.'

The phone went dead.

There was nothing else Maya could do.

CHAPTER 14
DON'T JUDGE A BOOK BY ITS COVER

Maya tried to imagine Mum coming face-to-face with a polar bear in Gran's kitchen. She tried to imagine what Mister P might do.

'What do you think will happen?' asked Maya.

Max shrugged. 'Perhaps it is for the best. They had to meet the bear some time. If they realize he is not just part of her imagination, it could be a good thing—for Gran anyway.'

'But not for Mister P. It would be terrible if he ended up at the zoo. We can't let that happen.'

Iris appeared all dressed up and ready for a night out. 'You're not still talking about that bear, are you? Poor Gran. It must be terrible when you don't know what's going on any more.'

'She knows exactly what's going on,' said Maya. 'It's you who doesn't know what's going on.'

'Off somewhere nice?' Max interrupted.

'Just to meet some of Sam's friends,' said Iris, tucking her hair behind her ears. 'He's coming to pick me up.'

'Are you going to introduce us?' asked Max.

'You must be joking! One mention of a polar bear and he'll think we're all mad and never want to see me again. You two need to stay out of the way, OK?'

Max made a rude face behind Iris's back and Maya tried not to giggle.

Max's phone pinged as a text came through.

'Uh-oh,' he said. 'It's from Mum. This could be trouble. Bear alert.'

'Oh shut up,' said Iris.

'Actually,' said Max. 'What Mum says is that she's not happy leaving Gran so she's decided to stay the night.'

At first Maya was relieved that there was no mention of Mister P. But then she focused on the rest of Mum's message.

'Is Mum going to spend the whole night away? I mean Dad isn't here either.'

'Looks like it will be you and me then,' said Max with a grin. **'Party time.'**

Maya tried to smile. She didn't like the idea of both Mum and Dad being away.

Max's phone pinged again.

'Now what?' he said. 'Oh for goodness sake. That's the last thing I need. The dishwasher at one of the holiday cottages has flooded all over the floor. Mum says can I go and fix it. Typical!'

He turned to Iris. 'What time are you going Iris?'

'In about 20 minutes, I guess.'

'OK, well wait for me to come back before you go. We don't want to leave Maya alone.'

Maya wasn't at all happy being left with Iris. She sat and watched her scroll through messages on her phone—which wasn't very exciting.

BUZZZZZZZZZ!

At the sound of the doorbell, Maya jumped.

'That'll be Sam,' said Iris rushing to the door. 'He's early. See you tomorrow, I won't be back until way after your bedtime.' She grabbed her phone and her bag and checked her reflection in the shiny toaster.

'But what about me?' said Maya. 'You can't leave me alone.'

'Max will be back soon. And you're all grown up now. You don't need me.'

Maya felt a wave of panic rush through her body.

BUZZZZZZZZ!
BUZZZZZZZZ!
BUZZZZZZZZZZZZZZ!

Iris winked at Maya. 'He's keen! Better not keep him waiting too long.' She rushed to the door.

'ARGHHHHHH!'

Iris's scream was loud enough to wake the whole village—which was loud, even by Iris's standards. Maya leapt to her feet, terrified. Iris could be a real drama queen and was quite capable of screaming about almost anything, but this sounded serious. Maya wished someone was here.

'ARGHHHHHHHHHH!'

This time Iris's scream went up and down and round and round and on and on.

Maya tried to face her fears and peeped round the door. Outside, standing tall, was Mister P, his paws stuffed in his ears and a terrified look on his face. Iris stood frozen to the spot, screaming her

head off.

'Mister P!' shouted Maya, running towards the door with a big smile on her face.

Mister P took a step forward and Iris screamed again.

'Don't worry about Iris,' said Maya. 'She'll be all right in a minute.'

Mister P pressed harder on his ears, but Iris wouldn't stop.

'ARGHHHHHHHHHH!'

There's only so much a bear can take and, finally, Mister P had had enough. He thrust his face forward so his nose was almost touching Iris's, then he opened his mouth wide, showing all his teeth, and

ROARRRRRRED!

That shut Iris right up. She crumpled into a heap on the ground and started to cry. Mister P grinned and looked very pleased with himself.

'You never told me he was real,' Iris sobbed.

She found a tissue in her handbag and dabbed away at her eyes, trying not to smudge her mascara.

'You wouldn't have believed us,' said Maya.

'*Us?*' said Iris. 'Who else knows.'

'Max.'

Iris looked shocked. 'Why the secrecy? Why didn't you tell us?'

'Because Gran asked us not to. She said Dad would send Mister P to the zoo.'

'Which is exactly where a polar bear should be. Imagine the danger Gran is in with this bear lurking around.'

Mister P curled up his lip and growled and Iris started crying all over again.

'It was Mister P who rescued Gran from the rip tide, actually,' said Maya. 'So imagine the danger she'd be in *without* him.'

'I don't want to hear any more,' sobbed Iris. 'You have to get rid of that animal before Sam arrives. Tell him to go away.'

'Don't be silly,' said Maya, giving Mister P a hug. 'He may look and sound fierce, but underneath he is really friendly—if you're nice to him. Gran hasn't had any problems with him at all.'

Iris struggled to her feet. 'That's because Gran has no idea what time of day it is, let alone anything else. Polar bears are not friendly. They are not pets. You wait until I tell Mum and Dad about this.'

Mister P hung his huge white head so his nose was nearly on the ground.

Iris pointed at him with a long blue fingernail. 'Go away Mister P. You are *not* welcome. You do *not* belong here. You should go back to wherever you came from.'

Maya couldn't believe what she was hearing She had no idea Iris could be so horrible.

Mister P raised his eyes slowly and blinked. Sadly, he turned, then lumbered off into the darkness.

'Mister P,' Maya called. 'Come back!' She tried to run after him, but Iris held her back.

'If I see that bear near our house again, I will call the zoo myself,' said Iris.

'You didn't even give him a chance.'

Iris turned away and took a mirror out of her bag to examine her face. She huffed with annoyance. 'I'll have to go upstairs and do my make-up again now. This is ridiculous.'

Maya couldn't agree more. Iris *was* ridiculous. She did everything she could to look pretty on the outside, but that didn't count for anything when underneath she was so mean.

A few minutes later Sam came and knocked gently at the door. Maya opened it.

'Hi,' said Sam. 'You must be Maya. I've heard all about you.'

Maya wondered what Iris had told him. Probably nothing nice. Iris came running back down the stairs and flung her arms around Sam's neck. 'See you later, Maya,' she said sweetly.

'But you can't leave me. There's no one else here.'

'We can stay,' said Sam. 'It doesn't matter if we're late.'

'Maya will be fine,' said Iris. 'Max will be back in a minute and Maya is quite capable of standing on her own two feet.'

The door slammed behind her.

And Maya was alone.

CHAPTER 15
STANDING ON YOUR OWN TWO FEET

Maya had never once been left alone at home. She'd never had a night without Mum and Dad. The house felt empty and shadowy. Every sound was louder and the air was somehow . . . heavier. Everything felt wrong. What if no one came back—ever?

She tried to tell herself that Max would be back soon. She decided to count to a hundred . . . then two hundred . . . then three hundred.

She told herself that lots of people lived alone. She thought of Granny Anne. She'd been living by herself since Grandpa Ted died. But

Gran was a grown up and nothing scared her. Maya wanted Max to come back. She wanted Mum and Dad to come back. She felt angry with Granny Anne for taking Mum away. Maya needed her. She needed Granny Anne to be OK. Even Mister P had gone.

Panic started like a small worm wriggling in her chest. Everything she knew seemed to be turning on its head. Why was Max taking so long? Why couldn't Granny Anne get better? Why had everyone left her? Maybe she didn't belong. Maybe she wasn't welcome any more. Maybe she should leave like Mister P. Perhaps that would make Iris happy.

She ran up the stairs and into the safety of her room. She tried to distract herself by making a memory note, but it didn't really help.

Abandoned

Where was Max? WHERE WAS HE? She lay down on the bed, and pulled the duvet over her head.

Darkness.

She heard a creak, a bang, and a thud, thud, thud.

Terrified, she curled into a ball, and tried to make everything disappear.

With a sudden whoosh, the duvet was pulled from the bed and the light poured in. Maya curled up even tighter. She didn't dare open her eyes.

Then she felt something soft nudging her back.

She heard a familiar sniffling in her ear.

She opened her eyes, just a little, to find Mister P standing next to her with her duvet held in his teeth.

'Mister P,' she whispered. 'You're back!'

Here in her room, the bear seemed larger than ever. What if Iris was right? What if he really was dangerous?

Mister P pulled at Maya's sweater as if he was trying to get her off the bed, but Maya didn't want to move. He pulled harder, reversing across the room. Maya's sweater stretched and stretched. Finally he let go and fell back into her table, knocking her memory box to the floor. The lid of the box slid open and all Maya's precious objects spilled out across the carpet.

Maya gasped and leapt off the bed.

Mister P started picking through the objects with his claws.

'What are you doing, Mister P? Leave those things alone. They are mine.' Maya's memory box was special. It was important. She didn't like it being touched by anyone else.

Mister P ignored her. He pushed at the objects with his nose, gently nudging a feather towards Maya. He looked up at her and waited.

Maya picked up the feather and held it in her hand.

'My seagull feather,' she said. 'Gran and I found it on the cliff where the seagulls nest every year. I'll show you one day.'

Mister P nodded as if he understood every word then pushed a small shell towards her. 'That's a mussel shell,' she said. 'You can search for mussels on the rocks below the lighthouse.' She pointed out of the window and Mister P turned his head. 'Some people like to eat them, but I don't like the taste.'

Mister P kept pushing objects towards her and Maya held each one in her hand, telling its story.

'Gran's old glasses!' she said. The glasses were cracked, wonky, and twisted and Maya laughed as she put them on Mister P's nose. 'Dolphin tried to eat them,' she explained. Mister P went cross-eyed and Maya laughed.

He pushed her the tiny bag of sand, the fossil, her first pencil from school, a candle from her birthday cake, the label off his suitcase. Maya's heartbeat slowly returned to normal. These were her memories. Nobody could change them or turn them upside down. No one could take them away from her.

Mister P seemed to be enjoying himself. He speared an old memory note on the end of a sharp claw and held it out to Maya.

'Careful,' she said as she took it and read it aloud. It was written in Gran's spidery handwriting.

'Maya arrives at Lighthouse Cottage.'
Attached to it was a photo of a very small Maya
with the family. Maya smiled. Mister P kept
going.

'First trip to the harbour.'

'First day at school.'

'First time on a bicycle.'

Maya grinned as she remembered Gran
running along behind her, trying to keep her
upright. She remembered the sense of freedom
as she raced off by herself, no one to support
her.

Mister P shuffled through to the more recent
memory notes.

'Gran and me, the beach and the sea . . . that's
when you arrived,' Maya said.

'Gran's last fishing trip.' She looked up at
Mister P. That note felt sad.

Mister P put the last one into her hand.
'Gran's last time on a surfboard.' That one felt
even sadder.

Maya put the note down slowly. She thought of everything that had happened since Mister P arrived. She thought of Mum staying down at Home Cottage. 'Things really aren't good for Granny Anne, are they?' she said aloud. 'Is that what you are trying to tell me?'

Mister P picked up the memory box in his paws and gave it a shake. It wasn't quite empty. There was one thing left. The bear tipped it into Maya's hand. Maya unwrapped her pebble from its velvet cover. She held it between her finger and thumb. Mister P gently raised Maya's arm and Maya looked up through the hole at the light.

There is always light at the end of the tunnel.

'Is there?' Maya said to Mister P. 'Is there really always light at the end of the tunnel?'

Mister P opened his furry arms wide, picked her up, and wrapped her in an enormous bear hug. When he finally put her down, Maya pressed her toes into the floorboards. This was her home, these were her memories, and nothing could change that. She knew she had nothing to fear. But what about Granny Anne? What if all her memories *were* disappearing. What if she couldn't stay in her home? Maybe that would be more frightening than anything.

She heard the door and Max's voice, his footsteps on the stairs.

'Mister P!' he said. 'I've been looking for you.'

'You've been *ages*,' said Maya.

'The dishwasher was a mess and then I thought I should try to find Mister P. Where's Iris?'

'She's gone. She didn't wait.'

Max stood very still. He looked angry and then sad. 'I'm so sorry,' he said. 'Have you been all right?'

Maya held the pebble in her hand. 'Can I ask you something?'

'Go on then,' said Max.

'Do old people get scared? Like Gran, for example?'

Max nodded. 'Yes, of course they do. Everyone gets scared.'

'Is that why Mum is staying with Gran tonight. So she's not by herself. In case she gets scared.'

'Maybe,' said Max.

Maya nodded. She dropped the pebble into her box and closed the lid.

'Maybe she needs a hug from Mister P,' said Maya. 'It helps a lot.'

Max laughed. 'Maybe she does.'

CHAPTER 16
ADDING FUEL TO THE FLAMES

The telephone rang just before 9 o'clock. Maya and Mister P were the only ones awake. Maya answered quickly so as not to disturb Max and Iris. Dad's voice was urgent. 'Gran's gone missing. Can you wake up the others. We need some help.'

'Missing? But I thought Mum was at the cottage with her!'

'We're both here,' said Dad. 'I came over as soon as I'd finished my shift. But Gran has gone.' Dad sounded all shouty and tense. 'She must have sneaked out this morning. It appears she didn't even get dressed so she'll be wandering around somewhere in her pyjamas.' Maya could hear Mum giving instructions in the background.

'Have you looked in the garden?' asked Maya. 'Have you tried ringing her? Maybe she's at the beach or something.'

'Of course we've looked in the garden and at the beach. And she's left her phone on the kitchen table along with a note saying she's gone in search of the missing polar bear.' Dad heaved a huge sigh of frustration. 'I've alerted the coastguard.'

'But the polar bear isn't missing,' said Maya. 'He's *here* at our house.'

'STOP IT!' said Dad angrily. 'This whole thing has gone too far. We need to put this polar bear out of Gran's mind. And we need you to help rather than adding fuel to the flames. You are simply making things worse. I know the polar bear isn't missing because there *is* no polar bear. But Gran *is* missing.'

Maya realized that this had all got way out of hand. Mum and Dad needed to understand about Mister P. She should have told them sooner. Now things were out of control.

Maya put down the phone. She was angry. 'Everything was all right until you showed up, Mister P. This is your fault.'

Mister P frowned.

'It's no good you sitting there and looking worried. We have to do something.'

Maya walked out of the kitchen, slammed the door, and stomped up the stairs. She tried to wake Iris. 'We've lost Gran. Apparently she's off searching for Mister P. Mum and Dad are in a stress and we need to help.'

Iris pulled the duvet over her head and said that as far as she was concerned, everyone could get lost, including Maya.

Maya slammed Iris's door closed. Sometimes she thought Iris would be happier going back to her family of four—without Maya. She tried to push the thought away.

'Max,' she said running in to Max's room and throwing open his curtains. 'You need to get up. Gran's gone missing.'

'What? How?'

'She's left a note saying she's looking for Mister P. Honestly, how am I supposed to keep Gran out of trouble when she's marching around trying to search for a polar bear that Mum and Dad don't believe exists. This is one hundred per cent Mister P's fault. If he wasn't here then none of this would be happening.'

Max looked quite confused. 'I don't think you can blame all this on Mister P.'

'Why not? If it wasn't for him, Gran would be safe at home in her bed.'

'If it wasn't for him, Gran might not be alive,' said Max. 'Give him some credit. Come on, get dressed and we'll take the motorbike and go searching.'

Maya pulled on her clothes, stomped down the stairs, and stood face to face with the bear.

'Grrrrrrrr,' Maya growled at the bear.

Mister P stared at her, his ears wiggling backwards and forwards.

'GRRRRRRRR. Do you understand me, Mister P? GRRRRRRRR!'

Max arrived downstairs in his old leather motorbike jacket. 'Once you've finished growling perhaps you could find that old motorbike helmet of Grandpa Ted's from under the stairs. Hopefully it will fit Mister P.'

'We are *not* taking Mister P. He'll never fit on your motorbike.'

'We are. It's time Mum and Dad knew what is going on. He can ride in the sidecar,' said Max, sizing up the bear. 'He'll fit perfectly.'

Max jangled the keys of his motorbike in his pocket as he walked out the door. Maya buckled on her own helmet and then set about putting the spare one on Mister P's head. It wasn't easy and Mister P didn't seem in the mood to help, waving his head around as Maya tried to clip the straps together. 'Will you keep still,' she grumbled. 'This is important. It will keep you safe.'

VROOOOM!

Mister P flattened himself against the wall, terrified, as Max started up the bike.

'There's no point in acting scared,' Maya said. 'You're coming with us whether you like it or not.'

Mister P did not like it, not one little bit. Maya had to coax him out of the front door and towards the bike. It was immediately obvious to her that getting Mister P into the sidecar was going to be a challenge, despite what Max might think. Max's motorbike and sidecar weren't what you'd call modern or flash. They used to belong to Grandpa Ted and maybe Grandpa Ted's father before that. Max loved them, but the sidecar was definitely not polar bear sized.

Mister P examined the sidecar suspiciously then lifted one paw and put it in.

'Come on,' said Max. 'You'll have to do better than that.'

Mister P put a second leg in, then a third, trying to keep his balance. Finally he heaved his last leg in then squeezed his enormous backside down onto the seat, his fur billowing like a fountain around the rim.

'There,' said Max. 'Told you he'd fit.'

Mister P shuffled around trying to get comfortable. Maya hopped onto the back of the bike and held on around Max's waist.

'Ready?' asked Max.

The sight of a polar bear in the sidecar made everyone stop and look. Wherever they went, Maya asked if anyone had seen Gran out in her pyjamas, but with no luck. No one at the harbour had seen her. No one in the village had seen her.

'Come on, Mister P. Do something useful,' said Maya.

Mister P raised his nose to the breeze and closed his eyes. Then he tapped Max on the shoulder and pointed up the hill with his paw. 'Hmmm,' said Max. 'Maybe Mister P knows something we don't.

'Perhaps he is using his sense of smell,' said Maya. 'Apparently polar bears can smell things from miles away.'

Whatever it was, Mister P seemed very

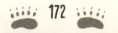

certain in which direction they should be going.
The exhaust popped and belched out smoke as
Max revved the motor, the bike struggling up
the steep hill with its heavy load. At the top
Mister P held out his paw and Max did his best
to keep in the right direction. Mister P held his
nose high as they rattled along, clinging to the
sides of his little sidecar as it swerved around the
steep corners of the narrow lanes.

They were almost at the main road when
Mister P held his paw high in the air. Max
slowed the bike.

Máya recognized this place. Gran had once brought her walking in these woods. They'd had lunch sitting at a . . .

Max pulled into a parking spot at the side of the road and brought the bike to a stop. There, sitting at a picnic table on the edge of the woods, was Granny Anne.

'Oh, there you all are,' said Gran as if she'd been waiting for them. 'I wondered when you'd be coming.'

Max and Maya looked at each other. Gran had a small pile of wild strawberries in a basket in front of her.

'Granny Anne!' said Maya. 'We've been looking for you for ages. Where have you been? Dad said you were out searching for Mister P.'

'But he's there!' Gran pointed at the bear. 'So why would I be searching for him?'

Maya's head was beginning to hurt.

'What *have* you been doing then?' asked Max.

Gran looked around as if she wasn't quite sure. 'I think I've been picking strawberries.'

Max's eyes widened. 'In your *pyjamas?*'

Gran looked down at her clothes. First she laughed and then she frowned. 'Oh dear,' she said. 'I must have forgotten . . .'

'Never mind,' said Max. 'Mum and Dad are worried. We need to get you home.'

'I don't want to go home,' said Gran. 'Not if those two interfering old busybodies are there.'

Maya saw Max take a deep breath.

Mister P leaned out of the sidecar and picked up Gran as if she was light as a feather. He wedged her in front of him in the sidecar then took off his helmet and put it on Granny Anne's head. He held on to her tightly with his paws to make sure she was quite safe.

'Polar bear hug?' said Max.

Maya smiled.

They drove home as quickly as they could with Gran complaining all the way. They pulled

up outside Gran's house just as Mum and Dad
came hurrying along the street towards them.

'Oh, they're still here, are they?' said Gran. 'I
thought they might have gone by now.'

Maya could see Mum and Dad's mouths drop
open as they took in the sight in front of them.
Dad put out his arm and brought Mum to a
stop. He looked at the bear. 'Let go of Granny

Anne,' he said in an overly calm voice.

Mister P lifted Gran and put her carefully onto the road.

'It's all right, Anne,' said Dad. 'Don't make any sudden moves and walk slowly towards me.'

'What on earth is the matter with you?' asked Gran, sounding irritated.

Dad pointed at Mister P as if he thought Gran might not have noticed that she was standing next to a polar bear. 'We'll call the zoo right away. There's no need to be alarmed.'

'I'm not alarmed,' said Gran. 'You are the one who is alarmed.'

'Don't call the zoo,' said Maya. 'Please, give us a chance to explain.'

Maya put her hand on Mister P's back. 'I think the time has come to introduce you to Mum and Dad,' she said. 'Out you get.'

Mister P pushed with his front paws, trying to lever himself out of the sidecar. He frowned in concentration and gritted his teeth, but he didn't budge a millimetre. In fact, he was well and truly stuck.

Max shouted to Mum and Dad, 'You'll have to help.'

Mum and Dad didn't move.

'Come on,' said Gran. 'He won't hurt you.'

Mister P huffed and puffed as he struggled to get himself out, but he was going nowhere.

Gran laughed and laughed. Reluctantly, Mum and Dad crept towards the bike.

'Take one paw each and pull,' said Max. 'Maya and I will push from behind. Gran, you hold the bike steady.'

Slowly, slowly, Mister P's huge body began to shift and suddenly, with a POP, he flew out of the sidecar like a cork and landed on the road with a bump sending Mum and Dad flat on their backs.

'Ouch,' said Maya, covering her mouth with her hand to stop herself from laughing.

The bear got to his feet and looked Mum and

Dad up and down. He held out a paw first to
Mum and then to Dad and helped them up off
the ground. Dad rubbed his back. Mum rubbed
her eyes.

'Mum, Dad,' said Maya, 'This is Mister P.'

They stood and stared.

'This is much more serious than I thought,'
said Dad.

'Anyone for strawberries?' said Gran.

CHAPTER 17
WALKING ON THE EDGE

Mum and Dad perched on the edge of Gran's sofa. They kept Gran's table between them and the bear. They didn't seem to be adjusting to the idea of a Mister P very well at all, but at least Dad had agreed not to call the zoo for the time being.

'I need to have a serious talk with Granny Anne,' said Mum. 'And I can't do that with a polar bear hanging around so could you two please take him out of the way . . . like OUT of the way.'

Maya didn't think she'd ever heard Mum so

upset. She decided she must still be in shock over the polar bear. Still, there was no point in arguing. Max and Maya got to their feet. Mister P followed.

'Where shall we go?' asked Max.

'The cliffs,' said Maya. 'I want to show Mister P where Gran and I collected the seagull feathers like the one I have in my memory box.'

'Lead the way then.'

Maya wasn't used to leading the way. She knew all the ups and downs of this coastline, but she never came alone. It was always Gran who led the way, pointing out insects and flowers; telling stories of Grandpa Ted's fishing adventures or daring rescue missions in the lifeboat.

'It's cool up here,' said Max. 'You can see all the way to the end of the earth.'

Maya laughed. Granny Anne had once explained to her that a long time ago people thought the world was flat and that you could

fall off the edge. She could understand why. When you looked to the horizon, it did look like a long, straight line.

A low-flying seagull swooped in overhead and Mister P ducked. It came into land close to the bear, opened its beak, and let out a loud screech.

'Pick on someone your own size,' said Max shooing it away. The gull took off in a flap of feathers. Mister P watched it soar away and dip down out of sight. He took a few steps forward and peered over the edge of the cliff.

'Come away,' said Maya. 'It's not safe. Only the birds can go there.'

Mister P looked up to where more gulls were gliding high in the sky. She could see his eyes following them as they spiralled around.

'I think it would be cool to fly, don't you Mister P?' she said.

'I'm not sure polar bears are built for flying,' said Max. 'You would need enormous wings to get something the size of Mister P off the ground. It's all about aerodynamics and polar bears don't have them.'

Mister P seemed unimpressed. He lay down, flattening himself out on the grass with a grumpy 'hurrumph'.

Maya sat down next to him. 'I don't know why Mum and Dad are so upset about Mister P. It's not as if he's done any harm to Granny Anne. Quite the opposite. Now that they've met him, they don't even have to worry that Gran is imagining things any more. You'd think they would be happy.'

'It's not as simple as that,' said Max. 'They might be upset because they're the last to find out about Mister P. They haven't had the chance to get to know him and it *is* a bit bonkers having a polar bear turn up on the doorstep. It's just one more thing to worry about. It's another complication. It's the uncertainty more than anything. No one can be sure what Gran may do from one minute to the next. Her behaviour is getting more and more unpredictable and it's hard to see how a polar bear will help, especially after this morning.'

'But he does help—most of the time,' said Maya. 'And they can't just have him taken away, can they?'

'Not if Gran has anything to do with it!' said Max.

'Or me,' said Maya.

'Or me, come to that,' said Max.

Mister P's small ears twitched backwards and forwards.

'So what do you think they are going to do about Gran?' asked Maya.

'I don't know,' said Max. 'I suppose they could move her to somewhere like Seaview Lodge.'

Maya stopped breathing. She knew Seaview Lodge. She went past it every day on the bus to school. 'They wouldn't do that, would they? It's

an old people's home. It's full of . . . old people.'

'It's a *care* home, Maya. A place where they *look after* old people. Old People like Granny Anne.'

Maya wrapped her arms around her knees and squeezed tight. 'But Granny Anne isn't *really* very old and she doesn't *really* need looking after.'

Max raised his eyes to the sky and shook his head.

Maya didn't want to believe he might be right. But once her thoughts got started, they gathered speed and everything started spilling out of her mouth. 'But if Gran goes to Seaview, who is going to look after me? Who is going to pick me up from school? Help me with my homework? Take me to the beach? And what about Gran's party?' Maya turned her face and hid it in Mister P's fur. 'They can't send her to live at Seaview Lodge. They just can't. And that is final.'

'You have to try to understand, Maya,' said Max. 'Mum can't carry on worrying like this. It's not fair on her.'

'But if Granny Anne goes to Seavew it's not fair on *me* either.'

Max was silent for a long time. 'But this isn't really about *you*, is it?'

Maya buried her face deeper in Mister P's fur. 'No one cares about me,' she mumbled.

'Gran is the only one who has ever cared about me. It would be better if I'd never come to live here. If Gran isn't around to look after me then Mum will have even more to worry about and then Mum will wish she didn't have me. If they send Gran to Seaview then maybe they'll have to send me away too.'

Max looked truly horrified. Even Mister P sat up and put a paw on Maya's shoulder.

'You can't think that, Maya. Nobody wants to send you anywhere. You're part of this family and we all care about you. But we have to recognize that Gran is getting worse. Mum feels responsible and when you're responsible you sometimes have to make difficult decisions. Mum needs to do what is best for everyone.'

'Everyone except *me*,' said Maya.

Max knelt beside her. 'You asked me the other day if old people got scared. I think it might be scary for Granny Anne living alone when things get so confused. She's given herself more than a few frights recently. She's a very strong woman and I know how much you love her, but you may find that Gran would be happier in a place where she can be properly cared for.'

'No,' said Maya. 'That's not possible. You are more likely to see a polar bear flying than Granny Anne being happy away from her own home.' She edged away from Max and snuggled closer to Mister P.

Max stayed silent.

'If Gran moves to Seaview then I am going to fly away with Mister P.'

'Good luck with that,' said Max. 'Running away from things never gets you very far. It's usually better to stay and do what you can to help.'

Maya got up. 'Come on Mister P,' she said. 'Let's go.'

She didn't leave Mister P in the boat shed. She took him all the way back to Lighthouse

Cottage. She didn't care what anyone said. Mister P was going to stay here with her.

Flying away with Mister P

CHAPTER 18
A BULL IN A CHINA SHOP

The next few days were a haze. Mum and Dad decided, after talking to Gran for a long time, that it was best to let the bear stay.

'Gran thinks that it is important for you to have Mister P around,' said Mum.

'Important for *me*?' said Maya. 'Why would she think that?'

'Don't ask me,' said Mum with a tired smile. 'Gran's thoughts are all a bit of a mystery these days. But as long as you are happy to take responsibility for the bear then he can stay here with us at Lighthouse Cottage.'

'Iris won't be happy. You should have heard her last night, going on about having polar bear fur all over her new black jeans.'

'Iris needs to learn to think about others for a change. Anyway, she's just got a job working with Sam in the fish and chip shop and Sam says they can keep the leftovers for Mister P.'

Maya shrugged. 'Gran and I can get him food. We've managed so far.'

'Maya,' said Mum. 'Dad and I are taking Gran to see the doctor at the hospital today.'

'Why?' asked Maya.

'They want to do some tests to help us understand more about what is going on.'

'So they can make her better?' said Maya, hopefully.

Mum didn't answer and Maya's stomach started to knot. Maya had only been in hospital once. It was before she'd come to live with Mum and Dad. She couldn't remember much about it, but she did remember not enjoying it very much.

'Maybe I could come and bring Mister P. He could cheer everybody up.'

Mum shook her head. 'I don't think that would be a good idea. He's more likely to give someone a heart attack.'

'So what am I going to do then?'

Mum smiled. 'Max is going to take you and Mister P to the glassworks.'

'Oh!' Maya had been begging to go the glassworks for ages. The glassworks was open to visitors on some days during the summer months, and now that Max had finished his first year of training, he had started doing glass-blowing demonstrations for the public. No one else in the family had seen him at work. Maya and Mister P would be the first. Still, Maya couldn't help thinking that Mum was trying to get her out of the way.

* * *

Getting to the glassworks meant another trip on the motorbike. Max was worried about putting Mister P in the sidecar in case he got stuck again, so he decided to let Maya and Mister P swap places. Mister P hopped onto the back of the bike without a moment's hesitation and wrapped his hairy paws around Max's waist. Max looked as though he was wrapped in a giant fur coat and could barely see out. As they sped along the main road, lorries peeped their horns, drivers waved, and Mister P grinned.

The car park at the glassworks was already busy when they arrived. 'Peak tourist season,' said Max. He handed Maya some money. 'I need to go and prepare for my demonstration. You go to that desk over there and get your visitor tickets and then go and look at the showrooms. I'll see you shortly.'

'Aren't you coming with me?' said Maya, worriedly.

'I can't, can I? I'm working. You're in charge!'

In charge? Maya looked down at the money in her hand and then looked at the bear. She felt a little nervous. She watched Max stride off towards the workshop. 'It looks like it's you and me, Mister P,' she said and joined the other visitors in the queue.

The man at the desk wasn't altogether happy about allowing a polar bear into the showrooms. 'Usually madam,' he said, 'we don't allow any animals.' He had a very precise voice that made Maya want to giggle. 'But as your brother works

here we will make an exception. You will have
to take extreme care because everything we have
here is *fragile* and *breakable*.' He said the words
fragile and *breakable* slowly and clearly as if he
hoped Mister P would understand. 'You will be
responsible for any accidents.'

Maya wasn't sure she liked the idea of being
responsible for Mister P in this fragile and
breakable place. Everywhere she looked, there
were warning signs.

DO NOT TOUCH

VIDEO CAMERAS
IN OPERATION

FRAGILE
PLEASE TAKE CARE

DANGER
FURNACES
IN OPERATION

'Stay close to me,' said Maya, 'and keep all
four paws on the ground.'

The main showroom
was reached by a long
corridor with brightly-
lit glass cabinets on
either side, each one full of
beautiful creations. Mister P
was so wide, his fur brushed
along the glass, making a long,
dirty smear. Maya hoped no one
would notice. Each time Mister P
stopped to inspect something more
closely, everyone behind him had to
stop too and soon there was a traffic
jam of people waiting and shuffling,
shuffling and waiting. Mister P examined
each object, his nose going up and down,
his eyes opening and narrowing.
'Keep going,' urged Maya. Mister P took
a few steps forward and then stopped again.
Maya watched his every move. She tried to shut
out the comments from people behind.

After what seemed like forever, the narrow corridor opened out into a large, circular room. Around the outside, behind thick red ropes, were shining glass objects of every shape and size. Some were tiny and delicate, others tall and elegant with colours swirling from the base all the way to the top. They gleamed and they shone. Maya had never seen glass like this before. She had no idea how it could be possible to make anything so beautiful. She was so proud that Max worked here. It made her feel more important than all the other visitors.

Mister P extended his neck to get a closer look. Maya pulled him back.

PLEASE STAY BEHIND THE ROPES

In the very centre of the room, on a tall stand shaped like a rock, was the biggest exhibit of all. It was a sleek black seal, balancing on its hind flippers, its body curling up towards the ceiling.

Mister P's mouth dropped open and he stepped closer.

'Oh no you don't,' said Maya, wagging her finger. 'You stay away from that Mister P.'

A guide in a smart uniform stood beside the glass seal, a large walkie-talkie clipped to her jacket. She waited as the crowd gathered round.

'So this is our most valuable exhibit,' she said. 'It was made five years ago by our master glassmaker and is a particularly good example of the Swedish . . .'

Maya stopped listening. Mister P was walking round and round, looking at the seal from every angle. She could see the glass animal reflected in Mister P's black eyes. She could see him trying to work it out. He kept edging people out of the way so he could get a better look. Maya tried to hide behind a tall man and hoped that they could soon move on.

'. . . and there is nothing quite like it anywhere else in the world,' the lady was saying.

Visitors snapped pictures with their phones and cameras, tutting as Mister P kept getting in the way. Once everyone had finished and

started to move off, Mister P stepped right up to the glass animal. He bent close so his nose was almost touching the seal's fragile whiskers. Maya couldn't watch.

'Who is responsible for this animal?' asked the guide. Everyone looked at Maya. Maya wanted to shrink into the ground. 'I must ask you to move the polar bear along, please.'

'I'll try,' said Maya. 'But you try moving a polar bear when it doesn't want to move.'

The guide put her hand to her walkie-talkie.

'Please, Mister P. That's enough now,' said Maya. 'It's not real you know.'

Mister P stretched out a paw and touched the glass. Everybody gasped. He stood on his hind legs to get a better look from above. His huge body towered over everything else and the other visitors ran to the far corners of the room. Maya could barely watch. She knew she had to do something, but she didn't know what to do. She tried to stay calm.

Nobody dared move. Nobody dared speak. Maya felt everybody's eyes flicking between her and the bear. What was he going to do? What was *she* going to do?

Mister P put his paws either side of the seal and raised the glass animal clean off its stand.

'Uh-oh,' said Maya. 'Put that down right now. You can't take it, it's not yours and if you break it then there'll be the worst kind of trouble.'

Mister P frowned and hugged it to his chest.

'Put it down or I will have to sound the alarm,' shouted the guide.

Mister P turned and looked at her and the guide's finger hovered over the alarm button.

'NO!' said Maya. 'No alarm. He's not good with loud noises.'

Mister P gazed into the seal's glass eyes.

'This is your last warning,' said the guide.

The glass slipped a little in Mister P's paws and the guide hit the button. A sound like Iris screaming filled the room. Mister P jumped a mile in the air then charged around, frantically searching for a way out. She could understand that Mister P wanted to get away from the sound, but the alarm had triggered the locks on the exit doors and no one was going anywhere.

Mister P was now panting hard and, in his panic, he **roared** at anyone who came near him. He was holding the seal high above his head, out of reach of anyone who tried to grab it. Mister P was holding thousands and thousands of pounds worth of glass in his paws and *she* was in charge.

'Don't drop it,' pleaded Maya. 'Whatever you do don't drop it.' She wondered if she'd be able to catch the glass animal without it breaking if Mister P let go. She felt completely helpless. She waited for the

SMASH

. . . but it didn't come.

Finally, Mister P seemed to run out of energy and Maya managed to pin him into a corner and coax him to sit down. His whole body was shaking. The alarm was still shrieking. People were still panicking.

'Get me something to block his ears,' Maya shouted.

Someone pulled a pair of headphones from their bag and Maya placed them over Mister P's small ears. His breathing started to slow.

Eventually, the alarm stopped and Maya carefully removed the headphones so she could speak to the bear.

'Please, Mister P. *Please*,' she begged. 'I know you can't really understand me, but you need to put the seal back.' She pointed at the seal then pointed at the stand where it had been sitting.

Mister P lowered his eyes to the glass animal and hugged it close to him. Maya decided it was lucky that his fur was so soft and his hugs were so gentle. She held out her hands and waited. Reluctantly, Mister P handed the precious animal to Maya who handed it to the guide.

A stunned silence filled the room.
Then everybody started to clap.

Maya couldn't believe it. She sat down beside Mister P, completely exhausted.

There were questions to be answered. Maya and Mister P found themselves surrounded by people in uniforms. But what could she say. He was a polar bear. He didn't understand. Polar bears like seals. (She didn't add that polar bears like to eat seals—she thought that might just make things worse.)

Max was called and arrived looking very flustered. 'For goodness' sake, Maya, I thought you could keep this bear under control?'

Maya felt terrible. She'd done her best.

Mister P looked as though he couldn't work out what all the fuss was about. He gazed at the guide without blinking. Maya wondered if he was trying to say sorry. Sometimes she wished she could understand what went on inside a polar bear's head.

'You gave us all a bit of a fright,' said the guide, kindly.

Mister P tipped his head to one side and the guide smiled and turned to Maya. 'I tell you what,' she said, 'Why don't I take Mister P somewhere safe so you can go and watch your brother doing some glass-blowing without having to worry? It'll be too hot for a polar bear with all the furnaces and we wouldn't want him getting restless again. We can take care of him out the back.'

Maya wasn't sure she could trust Mister P with just anybody. She looked at Max and Max nodded. They watched as Mister P followed the guide out of the showroom. It was a relief not to be in charge of him any more, but that didn't stop her from worrying.

The crowd of visitors chatted excitedly as they moved through to the glass-blowing demonstration. Maya took her seat in the front row facing three large furnaces. The heat filled the room and Maya pulled off her sweatshirt. She was glad Mister P wasn't here. It was certainly hot. She hoped he was behaving.

Max gathered molten glass from the first furnace onto the end of a long metal pipe and turned it slowly. He blew into the pipe and the glass inflated like a golden balloon. 'Ooooohhh,' said everybody.

Maya sat on her hands and watched. It was almost impossible to imagine how a lump of molten glass could turn into the beautiful objects she had seen next door. It was amazing to think that Max was part of the process.

The glass went in and out of the second furnace. The room got hotter and hotter. Max rolled the glass and started to shape it using a whole variety of different implements. It was very delicate and careful work and Maya was trying to concentrate on his every move, but she was finding it hard. The demonstration went on and on. She loved watching Max, but the more she tried to concentrate on what Max was doing, the more Mister P seemed to occupy her head. The bear was her responsibility. She should be with him.

Was this how Mum felt all the time about Gran?

Maya bit her lip and tried to focus. The object Max was making was almost complete.

Max gave her a special smile as he held it up for all to see. A small glass polar bear, frosty white with shiny black eyes.

The crowd got to their feet and clapped. Maya joined in. Max finished up and answered a few questions then came to join her. His face was red and little droplets of sweat rolled down his forehead. 'Did you like it?' he asked. 'It's not quite finished yet. It'll take another couple of days.'

'It was brilliant,' said Maya. 'You were brilliant. But could we go and find Mister P?'

'Don't worry, he'll be fine.'

Maya covered her face with her hands. 'It was scary in there with that seal and the alarm and all those people shouting,' she said. 'I didn't know what to do.'

'You did just the right thing. You kept calm and made sure Mister P was OK. There was no harm done.'

'Yes, but imagine . . .'

'Don't even think about it,' said Max. 'Come on, if you're that worried, we can go and check up on him.'

Max led her to a large shed behind the cafe. 'This is our staff room,' he said, as he opened the door and let Maya in.

Maya walked through the door and stopped.

Mister P was lying on the floor with a huge chocolate ice cream in each paw and a massive grin on his face. Maya wondered why she had wasted all that time worrying. Mister P was clearly having the time of his life.

'We know how to look after polar bears here,' said Max. He grabbed an ice cream for Maya. 'This is how we cool off after working with the furnaces. Fire then ice!'

Everybody laughed.

Maya and Mister P spent the rest of the day at the glassworks. Mister P was calm and happy once he had become familiar with his new surroundings and that meant Maya could enjoy herself too. She'd almost forgotten about Gran going to hospital. Almost . . . but not quite.

'Do you think Gran is home yet?' she asked.

Max stepped out of his overalls and hung them up.

'We'll call in on the way home,' he said. 'You can tell Gran all about your day—it'll cheer her up no end.'

CHAPTER 19
A KNOTTY PROBLEM

As soon as they arrived, Maya ran into Gran's cottage, closely followed by Mister P.

'Thank goodness you are here,' said Mum. 'Gran has been wittering on about that bear every minute of the day. Imagine trying to explain things to the doctor at the hospital. He doesn't believe us, of course. He wants photos as evidence. As if Dad and I would make up something like that!'

Maya and Max glanced at each other and tried not to smile.

Mum pushed her hair back off her face and

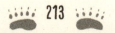

sighed. 'It's been a long day,' she said.

Max gave her a hug. He looked at Maya. 'Why don't you take Mister P through to see Gran and I'll help Mum make tea,' he said.

Granny Anne sat in her rocking chair. Her face brightened as soon as she saw Maya and Mister P. She chuckled as Maya told her all about the day at the glassworks.

'Like a bull in a china shop,' she said. 'I'm glad he enjoyed the ice cream. I'm not sure it is very good for him though.'

'Tell me about *your* day,' said Maya.

Gran rubbed her hands on the arms of her chair. 'Not as exciting as yours,' she said. 'The doctor says my memory is going faster than we thought. He says my brain cells are getting knotted up and that's why I get confused and forgetful and sometimes imagine silly things.'

Maya frowned. 'So can they give you something to un-knot your brain cells? Like some medicine or something?'

Gran shook her head. 'No. Sadly there is nothing they can do at all. My brain is going to get knottier and knottier.'

Maya thought about this for a few moments. 'Does it hurt?'

'Not at all. But it is a little scary—and rather annoying.'

Maya crept close to Gran and put her head on her lap. Gran stroked her hair.

'So is there anything we can do to help?' Maya asked.

'Actually there is something I'd like the two of you to help me with. I've decided to move house.'

Maya lifted her head.

'Move? Are you coming to live with us at Lighthouse Cottage?'

Gran laughed. 'And have all of you interfering and worrying yourselves silly about me day and night—no thank you. That's no fun for anybody. No, I have decided to move to Seaview

Lodge. They have the perfect room for me. I can even see the lighthouse.'

Maya swallowed. 'They have the perfect room for you *now*?'

Gran nodded. 'Your Mum took me to have a look.'

'NO!' said Maya. 'You can't go there.'

'Maya, I can't live by myself any more. I'd like to stay here—of course I would—but I can't.'

'So when are you moving?'

'This week. Rooms don't come up very often and I think it's better to go before I start doing anything too stupid.'

'Like fishing with polar bears, or surfing the rip, or disappearing in your pyjamas?' said Maya.

Gran laughed. 'Goodness. No! I hope I'd never do anything quite as stupid as that.'

Maya didn't say a word. She was starting to understand about the knots and the worry and the fear and the confusion. But it didn't make it any easier. She put her head back on Gran's lap. She liked sitting here with Gran in her rocking chair. She loved looking round at the nets on the wall, the photos, the trophies, the threadbare rugs, and the tatty cushions. This house was Granny Anne's life. It was Gran's memory box. She didn't know how Gran would ever survive without it, but she and Mister P would do everything they could to help.

There was a sound of clinking cups as Max arrived with a tray of tea.

'Stay there all of you,' said Mum looking at Gran, Maya, and Mister P. 'I need to take this photo as *evidence* for the doctor.'

Mister P gave his best cheesy grin as Mum held up her phone and snapped a picture of the three of them.

'That should make the doctor's day more exciting,' she said.

'I'm glad I can still make someone's day exciting,' said Gran, and she smiled—but it was a sad smile.

CHAPTER 20
HOME IS WHERE THE HEART IS

It took hours for Maya, Max, and Mister P to put the finishing touches to Gran's new room. They'd gone round Gran's cottage together, trying to decide what was most important. Mister P took down the fishing net from Gran's wall and rolled up the threadbare rug. Maya packed up Gran's photos and her favourite mug. They wanted Gran's room to feel exactly like home.

The trouble was, Gran's new room wasn't very large. Mister P covered his ears as Max banged in nails to hang Gran's surfboard on the wall. Mister P draped the fishing net over the top of the board, letting it hang down to the floor. It made the room smell of the sea, just like Granny Anne's cottage. Max carried in Gran's rocking chair and Maya placed it so Gran could sit in it and look straight out at the lighthouse. On a table next to the bed, they put photos of Grandpa Ted, Dolphin the dog, all the family and, of course, a large photo of Mister P. Every time Mister P looked at it, he pointed to himself and grinned. They put her toothbrush in the bathroom and some flowers in her favourite mug and spread shells along the shelf by the window.

Everyone kept telling Maya that she mustn't worry, that it would all be fine, and that Granny Anne would be happy in her new home. Maya knew it wasn't as easy as that. She knew it would take time for Gran to adjust to her new surroundings. She knew because she'd had to do it herself. She knew because of her experience with Mister P yesterday. She decided that she and Mister P probably understood better than anyone else in the family.

Soon everything was ready and they stood back to admire their work. Gran's new room was a masterpiece. Now all they could do was wait for Gran to arrive.

Granny Anne was a little unsteady on her feet as she walked into the room. A lady called Sarah led the way. She'd told Maya that it was her job to make sure all her residents were happy and well cared for. Maya liked her. She had been really helpful with their decorating.

Gran stopped next to the bed and looked around. 'Oh, this is lovely,' she said. 'What a beautiful room.'

She picked up each photo in turn and looked at it before making her way slowly to her rocking chair. She sat down and rubbed her hands along the wooden arms. She looked out across the sea and all the way to the lighthouse in the distance. There were a few boats out, fishing boats probably, chugging their way towards the harbour or out to the open sea. Tears formed in Gran's eyes and started to run down her face.

Maya snuggled up to Mister P. They'd tried so hard to make this perfect so Gran would be happy. Had they done something wrong? Had they forgotten something?

Gran rocked backwards and forwards, backwards and forwards. Then she stopped. 'Well it's been lovely visiting,' she announced, 'But I'm afraid I must be getting home. Ted will be back soon and we'll need to take Dolphin for a walk.'

Maya's stomach hurt. She clung on to Mister P's fur.

Max put his hand on Gran's shoulder. 'Gran, you know Grandpa Ted is . . .'

'. . . is not going to be back for a while yet,' interrupted Sarah, with a smile. 'And I'm sure Maya will take Dolphin for a walk, won't you Maya. Now I think we should go and have tea.

There are lots of people very excited about meeting you. And we've never had a polar bear come to visit before.'

Gran seemed to cheer up a little at the mention of tea. As they walked along the corridor, Maya fell back behind the others. She thought she'd never felt so sad. The sounds were strange, the smells were strange, and the people were strange. It reminded Maya of when she'd very first arrived at *her* new home. She knew how Gran was feeling and it was hard.

Sarah encouraged Gran along, telling her stories about the pictures on the walls and about all the activities that went on—outings and games afternoons, keep-fit and film nights.

'Sounds all right to me,' whispered Max. 'I might move here myself.'

'Here we are,' said Sarah as they reached the end of the corridor. She pressed some numbers into a keypad and the double doors opened and suddenly the air filled with the sound of piano-

playing. The room was crowded with people,
not all of them old. Some were listening to the
music, some were singing along, and some were
staring at nothing. Gran came to a stop. Maya
could feel her uncertainty . . . like walking into
the classroom on your first day at school. It was
fear of the unknown. Maya wanted to run.

The piano player started a jolly tune and
Mister P bobbed his head up and down and
kicked his back legs out from side to side. Then
he swept Gran and Maya into
his hairy arms and began to
dance. Soon they were
waltzing around the

chairs and tables and the whole room had come to life. As the music came to an end, everybody clapped. Granny Anne did a small curtsy and Mister P gave a bow. Maya blushed and felt very silly.

'Well, I can see who will be running our ballroom dancing classes,' said Sarah.

Gran, Mum, Max, and Maya sat down for a cup of tea while Mister P wandered around the room, happily accepting chocolate biscuits and making friends with everybody.

An elderly man with a long beard stood up and announced, 'I was once an explorer, you know. I went to the North Pole. This is the best specimen of a polar bear I have seen for a very long time.'

'Don't believe everything you hear around here,' laughed Sarah, 'but actually Wilf *was* an explorer and he really *did* go to the North Pole.'

Maya looked at Wilf. 'I think Gran might like Wilf,' she said to Sarah. 'She loves adventures.'

'I'll keep that in mind,' Sarah said and smiled.

Mister P's mouth was covered in biscuit crumbs and a lady in a flowery skirt was delicately wiping them away with a paper napkin. Tea was over. The piano-playing came to an end. Wilf was talking loudly to no one in particular about diving under the sea ice, but Maya could see Gran was listening. Maya felt a twinkle of hope. Maybe this would be OK after all.

'This would be a good time for you to slip away,' said Sarah to Mum. 'Sometimes a lot of goodbyes can be confusing. We'll take care of Anne and we'll ring you later to let you know how she's getting on.'

Mum nodded and made a move towards the exit. This was the bit Maya had been dreading. Gran had always been there for her and now she wanted to be here for Gran. How could she just leave her?

Mister P nudged Maya towards the door.

'Where are you going?' Maya could hear Gran's voice, urgent behind her. 'Don't leave me. I don't want you to go.'

Maya ran back and hugged Gran for all she was worth. 'We'll see you tomorrow,' she said. 'I promise.'

'But where are you *going?* I want to go home.'

'I'm going to take Dolphin for a walk,' said Maya, glancing at Sarah.

'But Dolphin is dead,' said Gran. 'What are you talking about?'

Maya didn't know what to say.

'You'll have to believe me,' said Sarah. 'She will be OK.'

Mister P nuzzled Maya towards the door again. A hundred eyes seemed to watch them as they left. Maya didn't look back.

She couldn't.

CHAPTER 21
TAKING YOUR LIFE IN YOUR HANDS

On the way home, Mum said she needed to sort out one or two things in Gran's cottage. Maya could hardly make herself go in through the door. It felt empty and strange without Gran there.

At the beginning of the summer, Mum had said that 'things' would have to change, but it wasn't just *things*. People changed too. Gran had changed the most. There were still glimpses of the old Gran, but nothing was quite the same. Mum and Dad had changed too with all the stress and worry. Even Max and Iris had changed with Max being busier and busier at work and Iris thinking about nothing except her boyfriend. Everything had changed and Maya didn't know where she fitted in this new picture. She wasn't sure where she belonged any more. She wasn't sure *if* she belonged at all.

She walked from room to room with Mister P. The door to Gran's games cupboard was open and Maya crouched down to look inside. She reached in and pulled out Gran's bag of marbles. They spilled out across the floor, rolling to the far corners of the room. Nothing lasts forever, Maya realized. Nothing.

She couldn't stay in the cottage a moment longer. She ran out of the door and down the steep path to the beach. She ran and ran and ran. Even though it wasn't night, the sky was very dark. She looked over her shoulder and could see Mister P slowly making his way down behind her. She ran faster. The sea was rough. Big waves attacked the beach with breathtaking force, the next wave booming in before the last one had retreated. The wind whipped her hair against her face and the salt burned her eyes.

She made her way up onto the rocks. The cliffs towered above her. She glanced over her shoulder. Mister P was close to the bottom of the path, but the path had disappeared into the sea and the beach that was normally there had been replaced by angry water. Maya realized the danger too late.

It was a big tide.

It was a stormy sea.

Maya was cut off . . . and she couldn't get back.

* * *

Another wave pounded in and flattened her against the cliff. Sheet lightning lit up the sea and distant thunder rolled in from the horizon. She and Mister P looked at each other across the water. Mister P looked terrified.

'Mister P!' she shouted, but her words went nowhere.

Mister P turned away and set off back up the path.

'Mister P!' screamed Maya. 'You need to help me.'

But Mister P didn't stop.

Another crack of thunder. Another wave hitting the rocks, covering her with salty spray. Maya knew she had to get to safety somehow, somewhere. And the only way was up.

She clung on to the cliff face as she climbed upwards, her hands and feet finding tiny crevices. She didn't need to go too high to be above the high water line, but she was freezing cold and she'd have to wait here for . . . what . . . two hours? More? *Time and tide wait for no man,* she thought to herself. She could see a slightly wider ledge over to her right. She edged her way along, her fingers aching, her legs shaking. She mustn't stop. She needed to make it to safety. She inched onto the ledge, turned around slowly then slid her back down the cold rock into a sitting position. She dared not look down. She dared not look up either. Chaotic lightning danced on the water and the thunder broke with a deafening c r a c k. She covered her ears and buried her face in her knees. Every part of her body was shivering violently.

At that moment Maya realized how much she loved her family. All she wanted to do was go home to Mum, Dad, Max, and even Iris. She wanted to see Gran. It didn't matter where Gran was or how much she had changed. She would always be Gran.

Thunder.

Cold.

Sea.

She tried to imagine her memory box in her hands. She pictured Mister P pushing the memories towards her—the feather, the fossil, the pencil, the glasses.

The rock was hard. The waves were fierce. The thunder boomed louder and louder.

'Maya, Maya, can you hear us?' The voices were distant at first, then closer.

Lights up above her.

Shouting.

Silence.

More shouting.

'I'm here!' shrieked Maya, cupping her hands around her mouth. 'I'm here!'

'The feather, the fossil, the pencil, the glasses
. . . the feather, the fossil, the pencil, the glasses,
the shell.' She repeated the objects to herself,
trying to remember the feel of each one in her
hand, trying to add one more to the list each
time.

'Maya? Maya! I can see you. Are you hurt?'

'Dad? Is that you?' It was Dad's voice, she was sure of it.

'Maya, I need to know. Are you hurt?'

'No,' squeaked Maya as another roll of thunder came in. 'C-c-c-cold.'

'We're coming to get you. Stay right where you are.'

Maya knew she wasn't moving even one centimetre. She could hear things going on way above her, but even when she tipped her head back, she couldn't see. They'd be rigging up ropes and making everything safe. She'd watched Dad do training sessions.

The feather, the fossil, the pencil, the glasses, the shell, the pebble . . .

Noises. Boots against rock. Metal.

'I'm nearly with you,' said Dad. 'I'm nearly with you.'

She saw his feet first, then his legs, and then the whole of Dad, right beside her.

'Dad! Don't be angry. I didn't mean to get stuck.'

'Easy,' said Dad. 'It's all right. You'll soon be safe. Let me get you secure.'

Maya was so cold she found it hard to move her arms or her legs. It took ages to get her safely roped up. Only then did Dad take Maya's face in his hands. 'My little girl,' he said. Then he hugged her tighter than she'd ever been hugged before.

'How did you find me?' she whispered.

'Mister P, of course. How else?'

Maya clung to Dad as they made their ascent. She clung like she never wanted to let go.

The top of the cliff was soon in sight and there, waiting, was Mister P, his huge white head and two hairy paws hanging over the edge of the cliff. His eyes were wide and his snout all wrinkled with worry. As she came face to face with him, he blinked hard.

'Mister P,' whispered Maya, reaching out to stroke his nose.

Mister P gave her the biggest polar bear grin ever. Slowly, slowly, they brought Dad and Maya up over the top of the cliff and unclipped her from all the ropes. Mister P lifted her up, spun her round, and then placed her down carefully in the middle of her family.

They were all here—Max, Iris, Mum, and Dad, all laughing, crying, hugging, and filling that painful hurt in her tummy with love she had never felt before.

* * *

Maya said sorry at least a hundred times. She knew she had been stupid. She'd taken her life in her hands and put others in danger too. But no one was angry.

She sat curled up in a chair, wrapped in a duvet with a hot-water bottle and a huge mug of hot chocolate. Mister P hadn't left her side since the rescue. He kept putting his snout on her shoulder and snuffling down her ear. It tickled and made her laugh. Mum wouldn't stop holding her hand. Dad said Mister P deserved a medal and Iris set about making one right away.

Maya said Dad deserved a medal too.

'Just don't ever do that to us again,' said Dad. 'We do not want to lose you, not even for a moment. We wouldn't know what to do without you.'

Maya smiled.

The phone rang. 'I can't answer it,' said Mum. 'It's probably Sarah about Granny Anne. I can't deal with any more today.'

Max grabbed it and gave Mum the thumbs up. 'Sarah just wanted to let us know that Granny Anne is very happy. She is playing cards with Wilf. She's also telling everyone that she has a big birthday coming up and that her granddaughter is organizing the party. Sarah asked if that was correct.'

Everybody looked at Maya.

'Wow!' Maya smiled. 'She remembered!'

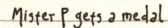

Mister P gets a medal

CHAPTER 22
FLIGHTS OF FANCY

Mister P was restless. For a few days now, Maya had been making preparations for Gran's party and Mister P was looking worried. He sat on the floor, his suitcase open, nudging the contents around with his nose. He'd added a bucket and spade and a marble to the strange selection of contents. He put on the headphones and took them off. He tried on the dark glasses. He put on the huge foam glove.

'It's all right, Mister P, it's not going to be *that* kind of party. No loud music, no flashing lights, no dressing up. Your bucket and spade is

all you'll need. And the mouth organ if you want
to entertain us.'

Mister P put everything back, shut the lid of
his suitcase, and fastened the catches. It was then
that Maya spotted a new label:

'I know who made that for you,' said Maya.
'Gran is up to her tricks again.'

Gran and Wilf had already planned a trip to
the North Pole. They had asked Mister P if he
would show them round—a sort of guided tour,
they said. Gran said Maya could come too if she
wanted.

Maya was learning about life with Gran at
Seaview Lodge. Sarah was teaching her to enjoy
what she called Gran's *flights of fancy*. 'As
long as Anne is safe and happy,' said Sarah, 'we
may as well enjoy her adventures with her.'

Mum and Dad found it hard to go along with

Gran's imaginary travels. They kept telling Gran not to be silly. But Maya found it easy. She was discovering that she and Gran were having more exciting adventures now than they'd ever had before. So far they had taken Mister P to the moon in a rocket and visited an underground city in a submarine with Wilf. She couldn't wait to discover where she might be going next.

'So,' said Maya. 'You're off to the Arctic Circle with Gran and Wilf, are you?'

Mister P looked at her sadly.

'Don't worry. It's not REAL.' Maya put her arm around Mister P and gave him a hug. 'You haven't got to go anywhere. You can stay here with me forever.'

Mister P rested his paw on his suitcase. He walked to the window and looked out. Then he walked back and looked at the label on his suitcase. Maya decided he was in a strange mood—even for Mister P. Perhaps he was bored without Gran to look after.

'Do you fancy doing some baking?' she asked.
'You can help me make the cake for Gran's party
if you like.'

Maya soon discovered that polar bears like
baking a lot. She also realized that cake-making
with Mister P was almost worse than taking
Mister P to the glassworks. Before long there was

flour and sugar and eggs everywhere. Mister P juggled the eggs before cracking them open, he stirred with his huge paws then stuck them both into his mouth and licked off every last bit of cake mixture. Maya reckoned there was more cake in the bear than there was in the tins.

And when it came to the icing sugar, it was like their very own snowstorm!

'For goodness' sake,' cried Mum. 'Will you get that bear out of here or we will never get this cake made.'

In the end, Max said he'd take Mister P out for a while. 'He can come and help me find the old deckchairs in Gran's garage. He likes it up there.'

Mister P seemed disappointed to leave the kitchen. With the dusting of icing sugar on the floor, he left huge paw prints across the wood all the way to the door. Maya looked at the huge

prints and smiled. It reminded her of the day
that she and Gran had first discovered Mister P.
It felt like a long time ago.

* * *

That evening, Mister P was even more restless.

'He's had too much sugar,' said Dad.

'He's too excited about the party,' said Iris.

'He was a nightmare in Gran's garage,' said
Max.

'Time for an early night, I think,' said Mum.
'It's going to be a big day tomorrow.'

Mister P gently touched noses with each of
them in turn.

'Goodnight, Mister P,' they said. 'Sweet
dreams.'

Before settling down to sleep, Maya and
Mister P went to the window. Maya threw it
open and looked out to the distant cliff. They
couldn't quite see Seaview Lodge, but they
knew it was there. 'Goodnight Granny Anne,'
called Maya. She blew her a kiss. Mister P did
the same.

Maya climbed into bed. Mister P rested his
nose on her pillow just centimetres from her
own. She liked having him there. She looked
into his big, watery eyes. Maya put her hand on
his cheek and stroked it gently.

'What's the matter, Mister P? Please don't be sad. Everyone is OK.'

Mister P gave a small sniff.

She touched his nose with her own and gave him one last stroke.

'I'll see you in the morning Mister P.' Her eyes started to droop. 'Don't forget, there's always light at the end of the tunnel.'

CHAPTER 23
LOOK BEFORE YOU LEAP

She might have been asleep for a minute or
an hour. She wasn't sure. But she woke with
a fright and knew something was different—
something was wrong.

She listened.

Nothing.

She listened again.

There was no sound at all. No sound of
Mister P snoring softly with his head on her
pillow. Just silence. She flicked on her light and
looked at the rug beside her bed. No bear. She
looked over towards her table. No suitcase. The

wind rattled around the cottage and Maya's curtains billowed out into the room. She walked to the window and stared out into the night. The beam from the lighthouse swept across the darkness. She looked again.

What was that? She was sure she had seen something. The sea was calm and shimmered silver in the moonlight. She looked again. A strange shadow drifted across the water.

She raised her eyes to the sky and gasped. It was the biggest bird she'd ever seen. Or was it a bird? She ran through to Mum and Dad's room and hauled them out of bed. Dad grabbed his binoculars and Mum her mini-telescope.

'Oh my goodness,' said Dad,
'OH MY GOODNESS!
That's Mister P!'

He passed the binoculars to Maya who held
them to her eyes and tried to adjust the focus.
Her hands were shaking.
Suddenly Mister P
swooped clearly
into view,
suspended
under a huge
pair of wings.
'Wow,'
gasped Maya.
'Mister P
is flying!'

Max and Iris came
rushing through to see
what all the noise was about. No one could
believe their eyes.

'It's Grandpa Ted's hang glider,' said Max.

'I knew that bear was up to something. Look at him go.'

'I hope Granny Anne can see this,' said Mum. 'It would make her so happy.'

'That bear is actually awesome,' said Iris.

Maya couldn't utter a single word.

Mister P soared up into the darkness. He gave one final swoop then rose higher and higher, raising a paw in farewell as the winds swept him away to the North . . . to the Arctic . . . to his home and his family. . . to where he belonged.

CHAPTER 24
ABSENCE MAKES THE HEART GROW FONDER

Granny Anne was seventy-five and Maya was determined her party would be the best ever.

Max had set up deckchairs, Iris had the beach volleyball under control, and Maya laid out buckets and spades for the sandcastle competition.

Gran raced down the path to the beach at full speed. Wilf followed behind shouting 'Wait for me!' Sarah came and Ozzy and all Gran's friends, including Mrs Ross. Callum and Lucy were there too. It was a big party.

Gran was in high spirits. She couldn't

remember exactly who everyone was, but that didn't seem to matter. The cake was delicious.

There was only one thing missing. Maya kept raising her eyes to the sky, just to check. She wished Mister P was here to join in all the fun. She wished he could see everyone so happy. To be honest, life was easier without a polar bear to look after, but the departure of Mister P left a big hole that was hard to fill.

As the day came to a close, Gran and Maya walked along the beach together. The water trickled between their toes as the tide came in. Maya told Gran all about being cut off and her cliff rescue.

Gran stopped and looked up at the cliffs and then smiled. 'Did I ever tell you I once tried to climb those cliffs. I think I got stuck on the very same ledge and Ted had to come and rescue me.'

'No, you never told me that.'

'Where is Ted, anyway?' asked Gran.

'Oh, he'll be here later I expect.'

They walked a little further towards the cave.

'I miss Mister P, don't you?' said Maya. 'He was a very special polar bear.'

'Miss who?' said Gran. 'What polar bear? Tell me more.'

Maya took Gran's hand. 'Once upon a time, on a dark and stormy night, a polar bear washed ashore on our beach . . .'

Gran listened to every word and she took a long hard look at the mouth of the cave. 'Shall we go and see if he is in there?' said Gran, hopping from foot to foot.

'Sadly he had to leave,' said Maya. 'He flew away on Grandpa Ted's hang glider.'

Gran laughed and laughed. 'You have a wonderful imagination. That is the best story I have ever heard. A flying polar bear! Fantastic! Will you write it down and give it to me?'

'If you like,' said Maya.

'What are we going to call it?'

Maya thought for a moment. 'I think we should call it *Me and Mister P.*'

Maya found it hard to believe that Gran couldn't remember Mister P, but maybe forgetting is sometimes easier than remembering.

They wandered back to join the others and everyone gathered around to say goodbye. Gran returned to Seaview loaded up with presents and cake and lots of lovely new memories to forget.

* * *

That evening Max came into Maya's room.

'This is for you,' he said, handing over a small

package. 'I finished it yesterday.'

Maya opened it carefully. There, inside, was the beautiful glass replica of Mister P. Maya held it in her hands and smiled. Max had made this for her. She couldn't believe it.

'Don't drop it,' said Max, laughing.

Maya touched the shiny black nose with her finger then placed the glass bear carefully on the table next to her bed. She could see the tiny black eyes twinkling under the light.

'I hope I'll never forget Mister P,' she said. 'And I hope he'll always remember me.'

SPLASHING ABOUT WITH BEARS

Mr P has no fear when it comes to the water, this is because polar bears are incredibly strong swimmers.

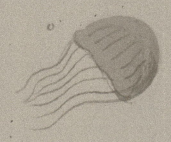

Polars can swim for long distances without getting tired, they have even been tracked swimming continuously for up to 100km. That's one long swim!

Have you ever watched a polar bear swim? It looks a little like they're doing a doggy-paddle. Their huge front paws propel them through the water, while they use their back paws and legs to direct them like rudders.

Polar bears make short shallow dives when hunting for prey, but they don't have to worry about water going up their noses because their nostrils close up under the water.

These bears can brave the coldest water because they have a thick protective layer of fat to keep them warm. In fact, polar bears are so well insulated that often they'll have a swim just to cool off.

MORE ME AND MISTER P FUN ...

Joe awoke, cold and stiff, to find the truck almost completely buried in snow. A glimmer of sunlight was just visible, which meant only one thing. The blizzard must have blown through.

Dad tried to open his door but it was stuck. The others tried too, but all the doors were totally blocked by snow. Joe hated being trapped. He needed to get out. He needed to breathe. He bunched up his fists and was about to open his mouth when the truck dipped at the front and two hairy windscreen wipers pushed aside the snow from the front of the car in a couple of hefty sweeps. Mister P's large face peered in and he waved with both paws.

The sight of the light and the sun and the bear brought an overwhelming sense of relief and they all gave each other high fives.

'We're stuck!' shouted Joe, pointing at his door.

Mister P set to work digging great pawfuls of snow away from the car. Before long he'd cleared Dad's door and then the back doors, and Dad and Mr Wildman jumped out and began to help shovelling snow. It wasn't long before Joe could lower himself out of the truck.

The scene that met his eyes was hard to take in. The world looked like a moonscape. There wasn't a jagged edge anywhere in sight. It was all sweeping mounds and hummocks and bumps of smooth and sparkling white snow.

Dad looked exhausted and Mr Wildman put an arm round his shoulders. 'They'll have the search helicopters out. We need to make ourselves visible so they can spot us.' Mr Wildman turned the two wing mirrors of the truck towards the sky to reflect the sun.

ABOUT THE AUTHOR

Maria Farrer lives in a small village in the Yorkshire
Dales with her husband and her very spoilt dog. She
used to live on a small farm in New Zealand with a flock
of sheep, a herd of cows, two badly behaved pigs, and a
budgie that sat on her head while she wrote. She trained
as a speech therapist and teacher and later she completed
an MA in Writing for Young People. She loves language
and enjoys reading and writing books for children of all
ages. She likes to ride her bike to the top of steep hills so
she can hurtle back down again as fast as possible. She
also loves mountains, snow, and adventure and one day
she dreams of going to the Arctic to see polar bears in
the wild.